ADVANCE PRAISE FOR YOU WILL KNOW VENGEANCE

“*WA Pepper writes a new techno-charged version of* The Shawshank Redemption *for the 21st century.* You Will Know Vengeance *is the first part of a fresh, new techno-thriller trilogy by author WA Pepper. Set within the confines of a prison, and the wilderness of cyber space, the two disparate worlds collide in a tense, gripping drama. It is a fast-paced, high-energy novel, that will keep readers on the edge of their seats. Whilst this book will certainly appeal to techno-thriller junkies, it is an easy-to-read novel for neophytes, providing a fascinating insight into the hidden world of hackers, cyber criminals, and the dark web. A FINALIST and highly recommended.”* - Readers’ Choice Book Awards (5-starred review)

***

"W.A. Pepper pulls no punches in sounding out the adversity and conspiracies affecting the world, and so readers will find this scenario as familiar as it is frightening...Those who pursue realistic thriller stories without being torn over man's inhumanity to man will find You Will Know Vengeance *a powerful saga which promises (and delivers) a fast-paced, action-packed series of changing scenarios. Part of what gives this story an especially*

vivid "you are here" feel in comparison to the majority of thrillers is Pepper's descriptive prowess, which reaches out to grab readers with sights, smells, and sounds...From dark web routines and Hackers' Haven to a gritty, streetwise analysis of social, political, and legal dilemmas, the story evolves on different levels to reflect the narrator's power and force...Re aders seeking a thriller steeped in too-possible worlds, undercurrents of society that exist today, technological conundrums, and the added overlay of interpersonal relationship challenges affected by conspiracy will find all these elements and more in You Will Know Vengeance. *This book belongs on the shelves of any library devoted to building a solid, exceptional collection of thriller novels, and is highly recommended for readers who can absorb trigger subjects in the interest of a complex, thoroughly absorbing story packed with surprises."* – D. Donovan, Senior
Reviewer, Midwest Book Review

***

"Pepper deftly amps up his engaging prison tale with perpetual threats.. .The author's crisp writing smoothly clarifies technical jargon with no sign of condescension; this creates a protagonist/narrator who comes across as an endearing, sympathetic journeyman more than a highly skilled ha cker... An absorbing, tech-smart tale that unfolds in a tense prison setting."
– Kirkus

***

"Readers will relish the ins and outs of Pepper's well-crafted dystopian prison society, swarming with cutthroat miscreants who will stop at nothing to dominate... Pepper's true talent is in scene development, and his pages are permeated with dark, gloomy tones... readers will be absorbed until the very last page and find themselves eagerly anticipating the promised sequel." – BookLife (Publishers Weekly)

***

"If you're into thrillers and smart anti-heroes wrestling their way out of tight situations, this book may be for you!" - Outstanding Creator Awards (WINNER – Best Writing 2022)

***

"You Will Know Vengeance *is a door-knocking, high-octane thrill ride, with a story that reads like a movie!"* - 9 Minute Books (WINNER – 3rd Place – Best First Chapter Contest)

Print and eBook cover design by Adrijus

Formatted by W.A. Pepper.

Published by Taddy Pepper (Publisher) at Hustle Valley Press, LLC.

Author photo by Taddy Pepper.

Danger's photo permission provided by his people.

ISBN 978-1-958011-03-4 (Ebook)

ISBN 978-1-958011-04-1 (Paperback)

DoGoodR

A Tanto Thriller

W. A. Pepper

W. A. Pepper

Hustle Valley Press, LLC

Disclaimer and Trigger Warning

The publisher and author advise discretion and caution when reading this book.

While this thriller is a work of fiction, it contains many of the dark things that, unfortunately, exist in our world: physical and mental violence, discrimination, sexual assault, suicide, intolerance, drug abuse, and neglect. Further, the sentence above is not an all-inclusive list of the potential triggers in this book.

If at any point you feel uncomfortable reading this book, the author advises you to stop immediately and seek the counsel of a professional that can help you. This book is not a call to action to hurt people, pets, or even yourself, whether that hurt is physical, mental, emotional, or spiritual.

This book is about overcoming those horrible obstacles, about diligence and resilience in your life, and about how evil will never triumph over good.

Finally, please don't cause yourself or anyone else harm. Love people and love yourself.

Taddy and W. A. Pepper

For assistance, there is a glossary containing technical terms used in this book at the end for your convenience.

Table of Contents

Pages were numbered according to the Paperback Print Edition of this book and may vary from various e-readers and formats.

Chapter One

My Damn Life

Abort.

That's what my gut tells me as I walk headlong towards the cop that's tailed me for the last two blocks.

In one hand, I have a cup of coffee. In the other, a magazine. While nothing is technically in his hands, his right hand rests on his service weapon.

My gut also told me *abort* yesterday when the most emo hacker I've ever worked with messaged me about meeting with a client about a job. During the whole nine-hour bus ride here, my brain and my instincts wrestled with each other. My brain very rightly pointed out that going after such a high-level government agency would put me on their radar. For over half a decade, I've flown under it, so why would I dare rock the boat now? That's easy, countered my gut, reminding me of the last thing written in the post, the nail in my decision coffin:

For DJ.

Even though my gut is currently winning the battle of wills, my brain isn't wrong: everything about this gig* points to failure. For the past couple of hours, I've walked all over this subdivision of Miami, Florida, overhearing pedestrians complaining about everything from finding a parking place to the overbearing heat.

And, somewhere along the way, I earned a beat cop as a tail. No one is as pissed off as beat cops. They're the guys who don't have an air-conditioned squad car and are just looking for any excuse to pat down or bust someone. Sometimes they are police that are starting out, but judging from the age of this guy, he messed up and got bumped down to grunt work.

When you also factor in the blazing heat and this sketchy black hoodie that makes me sweat like a whore in church, I haven't done myself any favors. However, if I break my stride, I'll throw any chance I have of getting rid of him.

Sweat drips from my palms to the magazine. My fingers itch from the perspiration. Unfortunately, I'll need to put down my coffee cup in order to pull this off. I just hope that my sudden shift isn't enough to be classified what the po-po call a *potentially aggressive movement*: anything that is a sudden change from a normal stance or situation.

I approach a standard blue mailbox, the kind you find on every other street corner, while still facing the officer. I might as well be an extrovert because I go so far against my self-preservation.

"Oh, thank goodness you're here, officer!" I yell, putting my coffee cup on top of the mailbox. He's not buying my act, because now his non-gun hand has moved to the radio transmitter on the left side of his neck. One squawk from that and any anonymity I have is gone.

From the inside of the magazine, I grab my map. It's not just any map; it is a tourist map. You know the kind, the one that folds up to the size of an envelope and, when you unfold it, there are ads for every money-grubbing tourist trap out there.

Even from five feet away, the officer's full body sigh has hurricane-level winds.

He probably would rather shoot me than help me guess where to find Gloria Estefan's star on the Latin Walk of Fame. That's part of the *serve* in *protect and serve*, I guess.

"Oh, sorry," he says as he squawks his own radio. "Have to take this. Go ahead, Dispatch. Over."

As he hurries away, I hear *Dispatch* answer, "Negative. That wasn't on our end. Over."

It isn't until the cop is completely out of sight that I realize my full body shakes like I am standing in a freezer. This gig hasn't even officially started, and I'm already so full of bile that I'm practically a Bourbon

Street

gutter. It's more than the encounter with the cop. I'm risking everything – from my freedom to my life – for someone I'll never meet.

And I'm doing it because I was just that age when someone stuck their neck out for this stranger and saved my damn life.

* This is the first instance of computer or techie jargon in this story. For definitions of terms, please click here (website forthcoming). Now we return to your regularly scheduled programming…

Chapter Two

Fanboy

Years Ago

I had left home with three changes of clothes, a half dozen VHS tapes, and a scrapbook. I figured I would live on the streets of New Orleans and sleep in unlocked cars that didn't have car alarms. Everything was working fine until the little bit of money I had ran out.

I'd heard the expression that you never know what you are capable of doing for money until you are starving. At the start of month two, I crossed some lines that I never dreamed I would: I stole. I robbed. I even stabbed a man whom I thought was following me. Luckily, his heavy coat took the brunt of the attack. He chased me five blocks until I got far enough ahead of him to jump in a dumpster and hide.

The stench of rotten meat and spoiled milk immediately flooded my nostrils. I lay perfectly still, though my heartbeat thudded like a bass drum. As it and my breathing slowed, I thought the man had given up.

I was wrong.

Something oozed from one of the torn plastic garbage bags onto my jeans, and I almost threw up. As I choked down my vomit, the man's foot-steps in the alley's puddles thundered in my ears.

"Hey kid! Come out, I just want to talk!" The man's high octave of his voice didn't cover his lie very well. I knew that if he found me, he'd kill me.

"Come on! Stop stalling! You want to act like a man, you come here and face me like a man."

He was right. I had been acting all tough and grown up, but I was still just a scared kid, now more than ever.

As the lid to the dumpster cracked and a streetlight illuminated me, I thought I was at least going to get a beating, if not a beating to death. Then, as the man leaned forward and I pressed myself, willed myself, to get deeper in the trash, the business end of a broom smacked the man across the head.

"You get out of my dumpster!" came a female's voice with a hint of a Japanese accent. "You want to use it? You pay me!"

"Geez lady, I'm just looking for a kid who—"

The solid thud of another hit to the guy's head sounded like someone kicking a watermelon.

"You can go look elsewhere. Go! Go!"

The lid slammed shut. The man grumbled a few choice words. Then his footsteps faded in the distance.

I let out a loud gasp, because I didn't realize I'd been holding my breath that whole time. And, to my surprise, the lid swung back open.

Then the oldest face with the thickest pair of glasses I'd ever seen leaned in and sighed.

"Damnation, someone is throwing away perfectly good white boys these days. Get out."

As I climbed out, I noticed she stood on a stepladder in order to spot me in the dumpster. This silver-streaked hair lady was so short she made me think about the cartoon Smurfs. She probably weighed about as much as one of those blue creatures, too.

Once I dusted myself off, I reached back into the dumpster to grab my Jansport backpack. Apparently, my zipper got caught on some debris, because all the contents of the bag splayed out on the wet ground.

"Shit!" As I gathered up my clothes and scrapbook, the lady in the green flowery dress grabbed one of my VHS tapes and looked at the label. I knew just from the broken plastic cover that it was Akira Kurosawa's Vendetta of a Samurai. It was one of my favorites, even though Kazuo Mori directed it instead of Mr. Akira, because Toshirô Mifune starred in it.

"You fanboy?" the lady asked as her intense dark eyes left the tape and studied me.

"No," I countered and attempted to yank the tape from her hands. She swiftly moved it out of my path, so I packed up the other VHS's and accepted that movie gone, a tax for my stupidity.

"Then what are you?"

"I am a Bushido warrior."

I'd never have imagined such a deep laugh could come from such a small person.

"You! You think you are Bushi? Oh, great white warrior! Ha!"

"Quit laughing at me!"

As I packed up my bag and slung it over my shoulder, I headed out. Then I noticed I could not move. The lady had a firm grip on my bag. I pulled. She held. This went on longer than it should have until she asked me, "Where do you think you are going?"

"Anywhere but here."

"Then you are selectively choosing to be Bushi." She let go, and I stumbled forward. "Because, if you want to be more than a fanboy, you must learn to live all of the Code, not just some."

"What do you know about it?" I countered in my most teen angst voice without turning to look at her.

"I know you now owe me your life."

Shit. I'd seen enough Bushido Code following movies to know that she was probably right. When I turned around, she greeted me with the same broom she used to protect my scrawny ass.

"You work for me now, fanboy. Now, sweep out my alley and then come inside for something to eat."

As my mind was trying to grasp how I had just gone from juvenile delinquent to janitor, I dropped the broom and glared at the lady who was staring at me from the doorway.

"How do you know you can trust me not to just run away when you go inside?"

She dropped her head into her hands and took a beat before responding. "One, because if you were going to run, you would have done it by now. Two, because you remind me of my son. He, too, was a little shit. And three, just because I don't trust you does not mean I don't have a use for you. Now, pick up the broom, fanboy."

As I picked up the broom, I asked her, "So, what is your name?"

"You may call me Mrs. Lin. I will call you Fanboy, until you earn another name."

"I don't want to be called fanboy."

"Well, it is either that or White Boy Fanboy, so you should quit while you are ahead."

Those next six months with Mrs. Lin would be the most educational of my life.

Chapter Three

Dangerous Words

I pick up my coffee cup and walk on towards the meet. This is about honor, not just freedom. As Yamamoto Tsunetomo says in his masterpiece Hagakure: *This is the substance of the Way of the Bushido: if by setting one's heart right every morning and evening, one is able to live as though his body were already dead, he gains freedom in the Way. He will succeed in his calling.*

My calling is to protect others, no matter the cost. Unfortunately, I'm three minutes away from stepping into either a tough job or a government bear trap designed to make an example out of hackers.

It's a steep price tag either way.

I set my meet with the client and my contact in a flower shop. Only rookies and people that want to get caught meet in a coffee shop or any place where they serve food. One, there are more cameras in there than in a bank because people will skip out on a check. Two, you get interrupted too often by wait staff and bussers. And three, there are more staring eyes than in a child's doll collection.

That's why, when the client got in touch with me, I insisted we meet at Trias Flowers, a florist on 40th Street. The plaque outside proclaims this place a 4th generation florist, expounding on how great-great-great-grandfather Pedro took what he learned in Cuba and brought it to America. That makes sense, since I am only a few miles from Miami's Little Havana neighborhood. I know nothing about my great-great-great-grandfather, except he had sexual relations with my great-great-great-grandmother at least once.

Through the store's glass front, the client shops. She's the thin blonde studying the white roses yet walking with a red one in her basket. It is a good sign that she is following directions. Sure, it is very 1940s cloak-and-dagger spy type stuff, but that doesn't diminish its effectiveness.

I've already walked the block twice. No one tails me, but that doesn't mean we are alone. The plastic pouch in my right coat pocket crinkles. Carrying this bag is an occupational hazard because, while it is a must-have for a hacker-for-hire, only someone planning to break the law carries one. If that beat cop had patted me down, maybe he would've just thought I used to have weed in it or something. I have no priors or warrants out, and I am not on anyone's Most Wanted list. I stay off them by being choosy about my gigs.

And then I had to go and get emotionally invested in protecting the person involved in the highest profile hacking conspiracy of the year.

That's part of my code, one that is greater than most governments: The Bushido Code. I am a Chukanbushi, a protector of innocents. I began exploring this lifestyle before someone older and wiser than me guided me into actually living the life, not just fanboying about it. Unfortunately, the role of protector sometimes means I put myself in more danger than a guy putting his head in a lion's mouth after bathing in barbeque sauce.

My watch reads 3:18. Two minutes until I enter. I can't tell if the sweat dripping down my brow is from nerves or the heat. The black cup of coffee in my right hand is just for show. I sip out of it every time I turn my head. Makes my watching less conspicuous.

This time, when I take a sip, I grit my teeth. La Colada Gourmet, the coffee shop two walking hours away from where I am now, does not play around. This blend is so strong and black it could absorb the sun, not that I am complaining.

Plus, stopping that far from our meet point gave me plenty of time to make sure I wasn't being followed.

Even now, I have my doubts that I am alone.

Something about this is off. It is gigs like this that require me to listen to my gut, which explains why my left eyebrow itches like ants are dancing in it.

I should be so far away from this gig that I'd be a resident of the moon. However, this is about DJ, and no one deserves justice more than him.

I check my watch: it is go-time. My contact who is supposed to introduce me to the client is late. Squirrel_Lord is a hyperactive hacker who runs his mouth way more than any hacker should, and he is supposed to be inside by now. Unless that Adderall-snorting goth with enough piercings in his face to hang a dozen sets of keys is hiding in the back of the store, this gig has a red flag so large it should fly over communist China.

The girl looks like she's a year or two older than DJ. The way she keeps chewing on her fingernails and pacing from section to section tells me she's nervous. She keeps glancing over her shoulder too quickly, sudden jerks and quick turn backs of her head. I can't blame her. A job like this either ends in success or goes down in flames greater than the Hindenburg disaster.

I'm only a couple of years older than DJ. While I've never met him in person, I know his picture from the paper. He's a minor, but factors like sealed court records mean jack-all when the Feds store files on an unsecure server. Well, not *completely* unsecure; I broke through the firewall after a couple of hours of penetration testing. In my defense, I was getting distracted: I had *The Silence of the Lambs* playing on a TV in the background.

I don't think there has been or ever will be a character with the same amount of grit and fear as Hannibal Lector. I kept thinking the actor was going to reach through the screen and bite my head off, literally. If a person like that ever existed in real life, well, I'd do everything I could to stay out of his or her way.

Everything from the rumbling in my gut to the ant colony on my scalp says stay away from this gig. Which is why I go against it and open the glass door.

For three minutes, I explore the stuffed animal section. Every florist has one. It is a complimentary sale item: get a stuffed panda, place a half-dozen roses in its paws and, boom, you've got an easy Valentine or birthday present. I pick up one of the blue-eyed white cats with the words *I'm not kitten...you're the best!* tattooed on its chest.

One clerk, an older guy with a head full of wet mop hair, notices me. His expression shifts from flat-faced and bored to a big, yet genuine, smile.

Man, do I hate happy people.

I can't just say that I don't want to talk. Unfortunately, to keep my cover, a conversation must occur.

Oh joy.

"Can I help you, sir?"

"Just browsing."

"Ah." The guy's nametag reads Cameron.

With oversized glasses and a mustache worthy of a western movie, he looks like a *Cameron* to me.

"Did you know that white cats with blue eyes are usually deaf?"

I did know that. I also know this is a stuffed animal, so unless I'm in a live action *Toy Story*, none of these stuffed animals can hear. I keep that comment to myself.

"Are you shopping for a family member, loved one, or for a certain event?"

"Just browsing."

"Ah."

He's not taking the hint. Fine. Either I play up to him or bully him away. I don't want to talk to him enough to make a lasting impression, but I also don't want him to remember that rude customer. I'd hate to give up my cushy life because, for a hacker, I'm pretty much out-in-the-open. It is tough living in the trifecta: rich, semi-handsome, and humble as hell.

"Would you recommend someone give a bouquet of magnolias or a marigold plant?" Yes, I'm asking because this store has the flowers grouped alphabetically, but it gives the clerk a sliver of power.

"Well, that all depends on who the gift is intended for."

"Why should that matter?" I ask. *Slow down and don't get defensive, T.*

"Well, is it for a resilient person or a giving one? Marigolds can survive draughts and thrive under intense circumstances, while magnolias are excellent supporters of other plants and are favorites of beetles because their pollen is high in protein, which they use for their food."

One of my favorite hackers is a die-hard Beatles fan.

"A marigold it is," I say, an idea forming.

"Perfect," says the clerk as he sifts through the row of the potted flowers and chooses one that looks like they should feature it on the front of the magazine *Better Homes and Gardens*. "Shall I put that up at the front?"

"I'll hold on to it, thank you."

As he passes me the flower and wanders to the front of the store towards the elderly lady that just entered, a hand from behind me suddenly covers my mouth.

"I want your money and your anal virginity right now!"

My hand instinctively goes back towards my attacker's face. My fingers wrap around a facial chain, but I let go rather than yanking the hell out of it. I turn to stare center chest at a black shirt with white letters that read *My Other Ride Is Your Mom*. I forget how tall Squirrel_Lord is. That six-six skin-and-bones hacker should be wise enough to know that the chain that connects his ears to his nose makes more of a weakness in a fight than a shocking statement.

"Who am I kidding? You ain't got either of those."

The daggers I shoot from my eyes knock that stupid smile from Squirrely's face.

We're not alone. To Squirrel_Lord's right is the client.

"So, I'm late, so whaaaaaaaat?" asks Squirrel_Lord as he raises his arms in over-exaggerated surprise. The rotating ceiling fan clips his knuckles, and he cries out, probably more in shock than pain.

The client looks me over and swallows hard. She's attractive in the quiet-librarian kind of way: her rectangular eyeglasses in a purple frame go perfectly with her red pixie cut. Even the freckles on her nose that appear to form the constellation Taurus add to her youthful appearance.

I wait for her to speak first. Feds never speak first. In my experience, if this turns into any type of negotiation, then whoever speaks first loses ground. If she doesn't say anything, I will head out the door.

The silence and humidity in here make me want to remove my black hoodie, along with my black wig, from my head. The less identifiable I am, the better. I may have six days of stubble and fake long hair, but you can never be too safe with your privacy and security.

The client straightens up. "You must be—"

"Call me Mr. Marigold."

"*Mr. Marigold*?" snickers Squirrel_Lord. "What, are we doing a whole *Reservoir Dogs* thing here? What's that make me, *Mr. Potted Plant*?"

"Does she already know your name?"

"Um..." Squirrel_Lord shuffles his feet.

"Does she know mine?"

"Naw! Naw, man, never, naw, I didn't tell her anything."

That's probably a lie but arguing in front of the client is pointless.

The client puts out her tiny hand. "Mr. Marigold, it is nice to meet you. My name is Michelle. My brother is—"

"No." I stop her. "Do not say his name or his handle." From my back pocket, I pull out a folded up black bag. "All phones in here."

"Man, you paranoid li'l sucker. What, do you think that we're being recorded?"

The look in my eyes must answer Squirrel_Lord's question, because his phone is the first one in the bag. Then the client puts hers.

"Aren't you going to put yours in there as well?" asks Michelle.

"I don't have one," I answer, sealing the Faraday bag that should keep all items in the bag from recording, transmitting, or even tracking.

"How do you not have a phone?"

"Don't need one," I say, pulling out my handheld scanner and looking around the room. "I need you two to stand under that purplish tree thing that's close to your height, Mr. Potted Plant."

"Ah, that is a Korean Lilac Tree," he says as he adjusts an imaginary bow tie. "Though it will thrive in a northern climate better than down south here. And just use my handle. I'm as real as they get!"

"Thanks," I say as we move under the tree. "You really know how to put the whore in horticulturist."

"Ha ha."

As everyone stands under this beautiful purple and green tree, I give it a shake and some petals fall on the three of us. I use this opportunity to sweep the purple petals off Squirrel_Lord while actually running the frequency tracker across his body.

"He's clean, your turn."

After a few sweeps, she's clean as well. Although just because I don't get a reading doesn't mean her equipment is not on. This scanner is good, but it is not a miracle worker.

"Shouldn't we check you, too?"

Her question brings a smile to my face as I hand the white scanner to her and spread my arms. She sweeps petals off me and scans me as Squirrel_Lord breaks the tension by pretending I'm bugged.

"Beep-beep-beep! You're a pig! I knew it!"

"I did have bacon for breakfast, Squirrel. Okay, someone, please tell us what fresh hell you are looking to procure from me today in ten words or less."

Michelle chews on the inside of her cheek as she counts out words on her fingers. Her eyes dart around the room as she does this a second time, possibly confirming her word count.

"We need to hold the U.S. Attorney's servers for ransom."

Credit where credit is due: rarely have I heard ten more dangerous words.

Chapter Four

Different

"In order to help DJ, we're going to need a bigger team." Sometimes I hate stating the obvious. Other times, it helps edge up my point. "And that's going to cost."

"I have twenty-seven thousand dollars to my name," says Michelle. She breaks eye contact with me, possibly ashamed because, if she's done her research on the dark web, then she knows this type of gig would cost at least four times that amount.

"Girl, I'll do this one for free." Squirrel_Lord squints as he runs his eyes up and down her body.

"Squirrel," I say as I shake my head because he hasn't changed since the Dallas gig, "what you're thinking you'll get in payment, she ain't offering."

"Girl, I'll do it for ten thousand."

"And you, Mr. Marigold?"

I, too, would do it for free, but for my own reasons. I admire DJ and have since before he hit the national news. His type of hacking, the inquisitive type, is powerful in our tight-knit community. He is a lot like me because, when you combine incredibly smart with intensely bored, you get a hacker that hacks just because he can. I want to tell Michelle that I read in an interview with her father that DJ started hacking young, like a hacking your middle school's server and changing your grades kind of young.

I mean, we've all done that, but at age ten? That's baller. Under the handle of DoGoodR, he broke government and various proprietary firewalls because *their code sucked.* I can't blame him. If you see a beehive, it may tempt the right type of person to hit it with a rock.

Before you attack the nest, you need to know how many pissed off stingers will come for you if you get in their sights.

"I want the kid safe, so show me the honey."

This request is two-fold. One, it adds to my professionalism. If I had a dollar for every time someone has screwed me out of a paycheck, well, I could afford to do this gig for free. And two, I need to confirm some doubts.

My screw up of paraphrasing a line from the movie Jerry Maguire brings a guttural yell of the same phrase by Squirrel_Lord, drawing attention to us, if only for a second.

"It's in here, hold on." Michelle rummages in her basketball-sized leather purse. She pulls out a gray oversized wallet. The kind that holds a checkbook. Pretending to be helpful, I extend a hand and hold whatever she puts in there. Two lipsticks. Two tampons. A travel sized pack of tissue. And the checkbook.

"Ah, screw it." She snatches a small, empty clay pot from a shelf and dumps her purse into it. She sifts through the various paper receipts, each crinkling in her hand. I pop open her checkbook. Her license and the checks match her first name.

But not her last.

"Here it is." Michelle hands me a folded-up bank statement from the Dade County Federal Credit Union. Sure enough, there's twenty-seven thousand three hundred and six smack-a-roos in that account. I note the account numbers.

Something to check later.

"Okay." I hand it back, because I now have what I need. "How long do we have?"

"Three days until the sentencing."

"Damn!" Squirrel_Lord's yell goes from a high octave to a low one, more disappointing than painful. "I thought he wasn't found guilty yet."

"We're too late to board that train," I add. "He pled guilty."

"How'd you find that out?" asks Michelle. "That's not public record yet."

She reads between the lines as I take a swig of coffee.

"Why?" asks Squirrel_Lord. "What'd they actually get him on?"

"Everything," I say.

You can find the answer to both of Squirrel_Lord's questions behind an Alabama firewall that caught DJ's eye in June of last year. Once he got through and found that it connected the computer to one of the most advanced computer networks on the planet, DoGoodR partied like it was 1999, and, coincidentally, it was. He set up his own administrative account so that he could install a login sniffer code, a keystroke recorder, which got him access to the Department of Defense servers in Dulles, Virginia. That gave him the chance to spend weeks playing with every system in NASA's disposal: flight design, rocket initiation, and even the communication system for the International Space Station.

The most powerful guidance system in the world was in the hands of a kid who wasn't old enough to own a driver's license.

Then DJ did like all of us hackers do: got cocky. Like serial killers, there is something deep inside of us that demands attention. Almost daring the Feds to catch him, DoGoodR posted a direct link to the backdoor to NASA on the dark web.

That pissed off the brass.

DJ got caught because he didn't scramble the landline he was using. He scrambled his IP address, but the U.S. Department of Defense has tools that a hacker like me can only dream of using one day. Now, ole DoGoodR is the poster boy for throwing the book at anyone that tampers with cybersecurity. Currently, he is the only youth that Attorney General Janet Reno is demanding that the courts prosecute like an adult.

It doesn't help that this year the hacker group DISRUPT is beating the hell out of every Department of Defense server on the reg to embarrass everyone from the President on down. Trickle Down Disruption someone labeled it. It isn't catchy, but every time those words hit print, the stock market drops faster than a guy after his ninth shot of tequila.

"Look, they got him for being nosey," Michelle says. "This isn't about getting my brother acquitted. There is no justice in this. He's just a damn kid that got curious. He's just turned sixteen. They're not just throwing the book at him. They're hitting him with the entire library. They're stringing him up for everyone to see, to warn others not to do what he is doing, and then they are going to throw him down a dark hole for life."

She's prepared that speech. It flew too easily. No stuttering or pausing. So, I hit her with something I've been preparing for the last few minutes.

"Why do you keep calling him your brother since you two have different last names?"

Chapter Five

Wake the Beast

"What?" Michelle asks as she steps back from me.

On the surface, she appears too young for undercover Federal agent work, but looks can be deceiving.

"Who are you, really?" I demand. I know extremely little about our *client*, so playing this card so early is risky. She could lie to me. I expect nothing less. Hacks are as much psychology as they are computer science. Hacks often are more about what clients do not say than what they do. And, just like computer code, all it takes is one glitch for an error to crash someone's system.

People lie to hackers-for-hire all the time. I'd go so far as to say that seventy, maybe eighty percent of each proposal or contract is a lie, either by omission or intention. The best of lawyers can tell when their clients are lying through kinetics, or the study of body movements. Personally, even if she fails this test, I need to hear her say why she's misled us before I move forward and get anyone else involved.

My gut rumbles. The time to bail is now. I pivot my feet and scan the perimeter. We are still in the florist's shop, but the store's wide-open floor plan and giant windows leave us exposed. I can't tell if someone is watching us from a car. I assume she's not wired, but I could be wrong. The technology for agencies is improving faster than a rocket heading into space.

Her not answering does not necessarily mean *Fed*. People get offended for any number of reasons. When you call someone out like I just did, it is best to wait for their response.

Michelle gathers her contents from the pot and loads her purse. She throws the strap over her shoulder and heads towards the door.

And that's a response.

"Michelle…"

She turns, expecting me to apologize for calling her on her shit, I guess. Instead, I reach into the Faraday bag and hand her back her cellphone.

"Have a nice day, you two," I say.

Okay, T. Move fast and get out of here.

Then a small grab, one that is kind, yet firm, stops me in my tracks. From behind my back, she puts her phone in front of my face. On it is a series of calls dating back to six months ago. Each one features the same nickname.

Boyfriend.

She clicks on a picture of them. Michelle is in a yellow sweater, and he is in black leather and thin sunglasses, looking like a generic Neo from *The Matrix.*

She's operating outside of the family to keep them safe. I would do the same.

"Who else knows about this? Who knows you're here?"

"No one." The steady look in her greenish eyes makes me believe her. She's not with the family on this mission. Something in her stare is something I know so well.

We live in a world without true justice.

When you live like that, the best you can get is payback.

Revenge.

Vengeance.

"Well, if we're going to help this kid, then it is time to wake the beast. Just no one tell her I called her that."

Chapter Six

Penalty Shot

We head to the Food Mart gas station a stone's throw away. It's a tiny one, but that is exactly the kind we need.

"Squirrel, give me a camera count. Michelle, I need two packs of gum that have foil wrappers in them. Not plastic. Not without. Foil. Something like Extra or close to it. I also need three dollars in quarters and at least fifty cents in pennies. Finally, I need a Reese's Peanut Butter Cup. Just one."

"Got it," she says as Squirrel_Lord circles the perimeter.

The noonday sky beats its hard sun rays down on my black hooded and toupee'd head as sweat trickles down my face.

Squirrel arrives with a report. "Two cameras outside. One near the dumpster and the other above the pumps. Nothing in this quadrant."

"Good. Inside?"

"Three, but I can see the VCR management is using to record. You want me to take it out?"

"Would you kindly?"

"Gladly." Squirrel_Lord glances around the concrete and finds a crushed beer can. He picks it up and shakes it before he pours rancid beer on his tattooed forearms. Then, glancing at his reflection in the side of the phone booth, he runs his fingers through his spikey hair, destroying its perfect points. Squirrel_Lord kicks his head back and smiles through slit eyes.

"I'mma…I'mma gonna do…it…"

When he stumbles into Michelle as she leaves the store, he yells at her. She bends his wrist back and kicks him in the nuts. Squirrel_Lord doubles over, calls her a less-than-nice word, and crawls into the store.

"Michelle, that was a great job of supporting Squirrel's acting."

"What support?"

Either she has the driest sense of humor or really did not know Squirrel_Lord was acting. I open the bag and take out two packs of gum, tearing off the clear cellophane and offering Michelle a piece. She takes it, as do I. Then I remove all the unchewed gum and put it back in the bag. The foil wrappers stay with me.

Michelle outstretches a brown paper bag with my requested change in it. I snatch up the bronze coins and flip them all over to reveal their printing dates.

"What are you looking for?" asks Michelle.

"Some without dents," I lie. The less Michelle knows about my process, the better off I am. Honestly, we need pennies dated before 1982. They are the best conductors because the United States Mint made those coins out of ninety-five percent copper, whereas more modern ones are mostly zinc with copper plating. However, I'm not telling this to anyone who isn't already in my extremely small band of brothers.

"Really?"

I don't answer. When lying, the less said, the better.

Sure enough, two relics, a 1940 and 1973, are in the pile. I wrap two decoy coins, shiny pennies from the 90s, in foil wrappers and unscrew the mouth receiver for the payphone.

Inside the receiver, besides circuits and dust, is a small space between the transmitter and the transmitter holder. It is enough for these pennies. I pretend to pop the foil-covered ones in, but then slip in my true copper ones. As I screw back on the cover, I hear the store's clerk yelling.

"You drunk asshole!"

"Thank you!" responds Squirrel_Lord as he skips our way. I wave at the clerk as he flips us off.

"How'd it go, Squirrel?"

“Wasn’t a problem. I just overfilled an Icee and tripped getting to the counter, tossed the thing and nailed the VCR.”

“Are you sure you got the actual tape?” I ask.

“Oh yeah! I ran behind the counter and shoved a handful of the liquid sugar directly into the machine.”

“You’re lucky you didn’t get electrocuted,” says Michelle.

“Who’s saying I wasn’t?” he asks, pointing to the trace of a black burn on his wrist. His twitching fingers remind me of the dozen times I’ve had the lightning chase through me. “Wasn’t the first time, won’t be the last.”

I pop a quarter into the payphone and lift the handset. As it rattles, Squirrel_Lord kicks his head back and laughs. “Say, Ta, I mean, Mr. Marigold, you making a little spy music over there?”

“Something like that.”

I dial a number from memory. There’s a fifty-fifty chance she is either letting this landline die or she’s checking it remotely.

As I reach into the brown paper bag and grab the last item in it, Michelle asks, “And what’s the Reese’s for?”

I spit my gum onto the candy’s wrapper and then unwrap the chocolate and take a bite. There’s something about the melty, smooth goodness of a chocolate treat during the day that cuts the tension. I offer the other peanut butter cup to Michelle, but she shakes her head.

“You’re giving too much of your candy away,” she says, then sends me a smirk. “Never forget that no good deed goes unpunished.”

Without further hesitation, Squirrel_Lord snatches the snack and deep throats the whole thing while the landline rings.

After the second ring, a machine with a simple beep goes off.

“Hey...I’m looking...for a place to...rent a...balloon house...got a kid’s party...so I’ll call back...”

Between each set of words, I shake the handset to give the transmitter in the receiver a chance to do its job. During World War II, the government designed payphones to handle Morse Code transmissions, even if their receivers got damaged. The newer models might not be able to do this. But that’s why I have a Plan B as well.

That's why what I'm doing isn't exactly Morse Code, though not that far off.

I call the number again. I clear my throat right as the beep goes off.

"Me again…look…kinda in a hurry here…got a stubborn child…he's real emo…"

Squirrel_Lord mouths something I could go do to myself sexually if I got much better at yoga.

"But…you come highly…recommended…calling again."

I tap the receiver and slap another quarter into the machine. Right before I punch any numbers, a manicured pair of bubble gum pink fingernails slams down on the part that hangs up the phone. The phone clinks and returns my quarter to me.

"What the hell are you doing?" Her narrow eyes and gritted teeth blast her impatience. "If she's not there, we don't have time to waste on someone not at home."

I grab the rejected quarter from the payphone's return coin bin and slam it into the slot.

"One, she's home," I say firmly, dialing the number again. "Two, she's smart enough to not answer her phone."

The phone's receiver buzzes as I await the machine.

"And you've worked with her before, right?"

"Wouldn't have this number any other way."

Mane-Eac's answering machine message picks up.

"She doesn't know if I'm compromised or not, so I'm following the proper channels."

"What's that mean—?

"Shh." I spot the dangling phone book connected to the payphone's base and flip it open to the back. "Hey…I also really wanted you to know that…Merrick's Magic shop is…open six days a week…they carry wands…and stuff…"

I hang up and count out the remaining coins as Squirrel_Lord belts out a paraphrased line from Bon Jovi's biggest hit.

"You're not even halfway there, woah oh!"

I pop in a quarter and reply, “Yeah, well, at least she’s still talking to me. Which is more than you can say after what you did on the last gig.”

“Well, after the gig, she almost castrated me.”

“And that is proof that God doesn’t answer all prayers with a yes.”

Michelle checks her watch, her impatience screaming rookie shit, even though we all know the clock ain’t our friend with this gig.

While they say that patience is key and timing is everything, it is experience that guides success. A man once had a rodent in his house. He bought a young cat from a pet store to catch the rodent. The pet had never had to scrap for its food, and ultimately the cat failed to catch the rodent. Then the man borrowed an old, yet experienced tomcat from a monk. The cat slept for days, letting the rodent explore, get comfortable. He let the rodent relax his guard, even dance around him and get close before he struck.

Back in reality, something in my gut tells me that there is a chance Michelle’s impatience is an act. If that is the case, I am not the tomcat in the scenario. I am the rat, and I must choose where to dance carefully.

“Alright, here’s what’s going on.” I hand the phone to Michelle and give her a partial truth. “What do you notice about this?”

“I saw you put two foil wrapped pennies in there.”

“That’s right, but we will get to that. Landlines used to work through circuit switching. Whatever was said into the mouthpiece moved through several switching stations, but only after the call got answered by a person or, in our case, an answering machine. Now, until about forty years ago, everybody had a dedicated copper wire, which meant you had to have a direct hookup to wiretap the line. Today’s newer landlines digitize our voices and send them through fiber-optic cables. Phone companies say this process decreases costs and makes everything more efficient. Bullshit. This allows for voice recognition software to record conversations for ‘quality assurance’ matters, which is merely a politically correct way to monitor and track conversations for certain individuals.”

“So, you put the pennies in the foil to what, scramble the call?”

“Digitized recordings rely on reliability and sound quality. Any spike of noise can cause a recording to reset on itself, kind of like how a buffered video restarts when the connection drops. In theory, a machine would erase everything I just said the moment that rattling occurred.

I don't trust *theory*, so that's why this is so damn complicated. First call had seven break-and-shakes. Next had eight. Most recent call had six. Miami payphone's area code is, ding ding ding, seven eight six. After seven more calls like this, our data miner will have this phone's whole phone number.

"I'mma gonna go pee behind that dumpster, keep up my drunkard appearance." Squirrel_Lord crosses his eyes and raises his index finger to the sky. "Back…in a minute."

I make my remaining calls and hang up the receiver.

In the thirty seconds it takes for Michelle to wander away, a shrillness of the phone's ringer, like a panicked alarm clock, catches me off-guard. I pick up the line.

"Hello?"

"Your messages are boring, T—."

"All day, every day, Ms. Magnolia," I interrupt. I've made it this far without my true handle coming out. Might as well keep that boat floating.

A grumble, followed by a sigh, floats through the phone line. "Who is Ms. Magnolia? Wait, you're with a client, aren't you? Damnation, we're doing shitty code names, huh?"

A rattle like a fork caught in the dishwasher rings out, and I recoil as a dagger of static hits my brain. *So, that's what the shake-and-break sounds like on the receiving end.*

"So, who are you pretending to be these days? Mr. Mulberry Bush? Dr. Daisy?"

I send a shake-and-break back. Mane-Eac cusses at me in Portuguese. I think she said *escroto*, which I think means asshole. Even if I'm wrong, I'm positive she didn't pay me a compliment.

At least she didn't hang up.

"This is Mr. Marigold here with some food that is about to spoil, and I need help catering an event in Miami."

She doesn't rattle back. I can't tell if she's pissed about the quick deadline or just pissed at me in general. Probably both.

"Anniversary celebration?"

"Wedding." I sigh myself because I know what is about to happen when I add the next word, so I grit my teeth, clench my eyes, and move my head from the phone's receiver as I say the next word. "Catholic."

Catholic is code for a government hack. If the Feds are listening to this conversation, the rattling on the other end of the phone will seem like overkill. Mane-Eac's response is the encoding equivalent of a thirty-second swearing bout that would make a sailor blush and cause raunchy comedian Sam Kinison to flee back to his former career: the priesthood.

I lean back towards the phone to speak but intercept another break-and-shake.

A ringing hits my ears and an invisible bullet shoots across the front of my brain. That means a migraine is building. Granted, I earned it for doing this to Mane-Eac, but the sucker still hurts.

She's pissed, but pissed ain't necessarily bad, though.

"Is it at least Union level pay?"

I brace my ears.

"It's for tips."

"I'm booked," her voice reaches me even with my ear removed from the phone. "Bye."

I've got one shot to change her mind. Better make it perfect.

"Wait. It's a penalty shot for doing good deeds."

I hope she catches my two-fold reference to both DJ's handle – DoGoodR – and our last job together. The one where Squirrel_Lord showed what he was really made of.

Chapter Seven

Mostly Harmless

Last Year

Mane-Eac, Squirrel_Lord, and I hacked, downloaded, and then crashed the servers for the Yamaguchi-gumi, the largest Japanese mob, on behalf of the Kazakhstan mob. Yes, I know one mob is as bad as another, but their money spent well. After the gig in Dallas, our contact, a man with a face so weathered it looked like a horse saddle left out in the rain, brought out the finest vodka I've ever ingested. His name was Sagdiyev Kalashnikov. If you asked about his relation to one of the most dependable automatic weapons on the planet, he would shrug and say that his mother was never picky with her lovers-slash-arms dealers. He had a beard so heavy it would make Santa Claus look clean-shaven, and he carried with him two large silver briefcases when we finished the gig. These were the kind that you expect to see in spy movies, the kind with combination dials on the side and so thick they could probably stop a fifty-caliber bullet.

After we completed the gig, Sagdiyev opened the first and paid us two hundred thousand U.S. dollars in gold bars. I didn't want to tell him it would be a bastard to deposit or cash. Days later, I found a currency trader that wanted gold much easier than I initially thought. In the second case were four bottles of Moskovskaya vodka, carefully inset in slots on the case. Each bottle had a layer of dust over it that was so thick you could practically see Stalin's fingerprints on them. Sagdiyev withdrew one from the case with the ease and precision that a doctor would probably take when delivering a baby, wiping off the dust to reveal a green label covered in Russian. According to Sagdiyev, even though the company had produced extremely good vodka for over a hundred years, only the stuff made before 1930 was "good" because after that the company had "Americanized" their recipe.

Blasphemy comes in all forms, I guess.

From the bottom of the case, Sagdiyev withdrew four crystal shot glasses. He called them stopkas or rumkas or something. The excessive amounts of vodka that followed have clouded my recollection of their true names.

*Sagdiyev handed each of us a full stopka of the Moskovskaya vodka. We raised them in a toast as he said "*Za Nas,*" which we repeated, even though we didn't know what it meant, and downed the shot. The vodka, despite being stored in that case, was ice cold. There must've been a hidden cooling compartment or something. It slid down my throat with ease, like someone broke open a thermometer and poured an odorless and virtually tasteless mercury that immediately bypassed my stomach and went straight to my brain. Before I noticed, someone had refilled my stopka. Sagdiyev held out another toast and said, "*Za zdorovie,*" which we repeated and then downed the shot again.*

The haziness of the night began. I remember Squirrel_Lord taking the first empty bottle from the floor and trying to play it like a jug in a hillbilly band. Sagdiyev screamed at him something in Russian or another language that sounded equally gruff and demanded Squirrely take a "penalty shot" for disrespecting the empty bottle. That "penalty shot" was, in actuality, an entire glass of vodka.

We shot vodka until three bottles were empty and respectfully placed on the floor.

I was curled up into a ball on the couch, hugging a pillow between my legs, doing everything I could to not look at the swirling ceiling. Squirrel_Lord, fueled with liquid courage, stumbled over to Mane-Eac, and tried his best pickup lines, before going down in flames. It all might have been fine until he'd gotten all liquor loony.

"Look, we've still got the data from the Yamaguchi-gumi, right? So, I was thinking, there's an offshoot of their gang that I have contact with that runs whores between the two. He could set up a meet."

"No, moron," she said, the topic sobering her up and resulting in a stoic response void of any drunken slurs. "No double dealing."

"It's not that, girl," countered Squirrel_Lord, as he towered his tall Jack Skellington body over her five-foot-three figure. "It's leaving money on the table. Sagdiyev already said that his employer doesn't want it."

"I said no."

I don't know whether it was the vodka-fueled idea or that Mane-Eac shot down his advance with laser-pointed precision, but Squirrely punched the wall so hard next to Mane-Eac's head that the drywall cracked. When he withdrew his hand, it covered her yellow leather coat in dusty white chunks.

"Girl, you ain't got no sack."

I'd only known Mane-Eac about two years at that point, but even I knew better than to push her into a corner to prove a point. She'd turned down twice as many jobs as I asked of her. You had a better chance of convincing Satan to give you back your soul than convincing Mane_Eac to do something she didn't want to do.

Mane-Eac rose from her chair and shoved her left hand down the front of his pants. The smile and flashy eyes on Squirrel_Lord's face morphed into a wide-eyed grimace. From his throat, a yelp that one might expect from a scared puppy trickled out.

"Squirrel, let me tell you all about sack. It's nothing but labia that holds your weakest vulnerability just enough outside of your body for ladies like me to protect themselves from advances from creeps like you. Yep, this sack you are so proud of has these round Whopper candy-sized orbs, or in your case, tiny pellets, that are extremely sensitive to pain and don't like it when I do this…"

If this was a horror movie, the noise that blasted from Squirrel_Lord would require Jamie Lee Curtis to hand over her crown for being the best Scream Queen in cinema. As Squirrel_Lord balled up his fists to strike, something in Mane-Eac's posture shifted. Whatever she did or however she moved her hands got the point across because Squirrely whelped and dropped into the fetal position as she let go.

"You don't create two enemies in one battle. You do the job you were paid to do. Anything else is white noise. So, yeah, I know a lot about sack, brocha."

After she let go, Mane-Eac stepped back and planted her feet, ready for whatever Squirrely might come back with.

While Mane-Eac wasn't a practicing Bushi like me, in that moment, she reminded me of the leader of the 47 Ronin Ōishi who once said once you know what you want, be prepared to sacrifice everything to achieve it.

Luckily, Squirrel_Lord took the heavy-gripped hint, crawled up from the ground, and dusted the drywall off himself. I leaned over and asked Mane-Eac if she was okay.

"He's mostly harmless." Her response started with a chuckle, then ended with a hard swallow. "He's no Epic_Chaos."

I eek out, "Ain't that the truth;" even just the mention of that a-hole's name turned my stomach. Then, like good little partiers, we finished the last bottle. I awoke in a bathtub with a small garbage can in my lap and the oddest hangover I've ever had: no headache at all, yet my kidneys throbbed like there was a nightclub still partying in them.

Chapter Eight

Silo

Now, as I pull back from that memory and stand at a payphone outside a gas station in Miami's Little Havana, I wonder just how much time has passed since I said that line about *good deeds* to Mane-Eac. The static on the line gives a slight buzzing, which may mean I am about to hear a dial tone.

She's won't risk anything over a long shot.

Sensing she's already hung up on me, I move the phone from my ear.

"Fine, you son of a bitch, I'm in. Oh eight hundred."

A click and the dial tone follow. As I hang up the receiver, I rub my scruffy peach fuzz of a beard and crack a small smile.

Now, we have a chance of this working.

Michelle grabs my arm so hard it turns me around. "So, what's going on?"

"She'll be here tomorrow. Until then, we've got a lot of gear to assemble."

"Yeah, there's just one issue with that," she says.

No one has ever used the word issue *for something positive.*

"And that is?" I ask.

"It's going to have to be a smooth silo gig."

If someone had a Richter Scale set for this exact spot, the intensity that Squirrel_Lord shouted a word that rhymes with *duck* would've registered a 4.5-level earthquake.

Chapter Nine

From Impossible to Insane

"I'm sure DJ would agree that there are few things worse than a smooth silo gig," I say to myself as I tear at my scalp in this heat.

The worst thing a hacker can hear about a gig is that it is a smooth silo. When silo comes into play, it means you cannot access it from an outside point. It is like how you can access your bank account and see what money you have in an account from your computer at home. To get actual cash in your hands, you must use an ATM or go to a branch of your bank. That's silo.

Now, when a job is a *smooth silo*, that means that not only do you have to do everything at the ATM, but you must hack the damn ATM with its own software.

It's a poor analogy because, honestly, it is easy to hack an ATM: ninety percent of them run on busted operating systems. A child could hack them with some free open-source software on a flash drive in thirty seconds. Allegedly, of course.

And now, Michelle says we can't even bring our own software.

"Impossible." I take one of my remaining quarters and slam it into the payphone's slot, then push my anger out through my fingertips as I stab each digit on the keypad.

Michelle asks, "Who are you calling?"

"Calling Ms. Magnolia back, canceling the gig."

"You can't do that!" She reaches her small hand towards the payphone, but I rotate to block her advance. "DJ will spend the rest of his life in prison!"

"And there's not a damn thing we can do about that."

Then, from above the phone, comes a long, slender set of fingers with fingernails painted so black that it initially looks like an incoming eclipse. Squirrel_Lord has the height and reach that he could easily hang up the phone. Instead, he takes a beat. Squirrely does something I'd never expect from someone as equally *macho* and *emo* as him.

He places his hand on mine so delicately that I hardly notice his touch until I feel a slight bit of heat, like that from a distant fire, warming my hand.

"Mr. Marigold, we can do this."

I, too, take a moment. After I place the phone on its hook, I study Squirrel_Lord's face. His eyes, normally a deep blue that borders on a shade of black, are red, as if they are holding back tears. Part of me wonders if he is acting, but the optimist in me needs to know more.

That's when it hits me: he needs this for more than just the money.

"Squirrely, what aren't you telling me?"

"Nah, man." He sniffs and wipes his nose on his arm, trying to play off this moment. "I just believe in this hack."

"No. No, you don't. And, even if you do, there's more to it. You're holding out."

"Nah, it's just that, DJ is one of us, man. He's the government's whipping boy. They consider him Public Enemy #1."

"Squirrel_Lord..."

"Look, DJ's a damn kid. He hacked NASA. Screw jail time. Give the kid a job, am I right?"

"Fine, if you won't tell me, then I'm out of here." I unscrew the phone's mouthpiece, retrieve the pennies, and screw the top back on. "I'll get in touch with Ms. Magnolia on my own."

"Look, man, it's that...well...I owe someone."

"That's not my problem."

I make it five steps away when Squirrel_Lord yells out a phrase that is worse than *I'm from the government, and I'm here to help.*

"I owe Barca."

If Squirrel_Lord would have said he sold his soul to the devil and needed to complete this job to get it back, I might have slowed my stride, but kept going.

Those three words stop my stride like an invisible wall.

Shit.

"Who is Barca?" asks Michelle.

I've worked for that asshole before. I've also been betrayed by that asshole before. Barca is the human equivalent of napalm: a mixture of sticky hate that completely smothers everything he touches in fire while he melts you and everything around you into nothingness.

Not that I feel inclined to share that with either Michelle or Squirrel_Lord.

This gig just shifted from impossible to insane.

Chapter Ten

Harder Things

"I need time," I say and turn around, not wanting any comments from the peanut gallery.

"DJ doesn't have time for you to hesitate," counters Michelle.

That's exactly what a Fed would say.

"Meet me at the Metro-Dade Cultural Center parking garage. I'll reach out to Squirrely with the time."

Squirrel_Lord yells, "You're just a coward!"

I ignore the prod and disappear down an alley before running two blocks to lose any potential tails. For the rest of the day, I run scenarios of how this gig might go, fixating mostly on how it can go wrong, attempting to predict ways around what I can't fix.

I contact Mane-Eac the same way I did at the gas station. The payphone rings.

"So, just how dangerous is this gig?" she asks.

I like a woman that gets right to the point.

"I'd say the wedding party is...rowdy."

Mane-Eac's sigh stretches out like silly putty in my ear.

"T, er, Mr. Whatever plant it was, are you in or out?"

I chew my lip and answer before my mind and gut get into a shouting match with each other.

"In."

"If I say no, are you still going to do it?"

"Yes."

"You'll have a great chance of dropping a platter and getting fired if I'm not involved."

"I'm not as bad a waiter as you remember."

"Maybe...curse your big heart...fine, I'm in."

For the remainder of the conversation, Mane-Eac never backtracks and bails. When she says onboard, Mane-Eac means it. She agrees everyone should help brainstorm for the gig itself but insists she and I should have our own contingency plan just in case. And, even though we hammer out those plans, we're going to need the luck of the Irish if the Feds are involved.

But there's one more thing even Mane-Eac can't know about, because just the knowledge of it going in could get everyone killed.

The next day, in the Metro-Dade Cultural Center parking garage, Squirrel_Lord spills the beans. We meet there because parking garages have multiple exits for a person on foot and the background noise from the street, incoming wind, and cars wheeling in-and-out of tight parking spaces kill any listening device audio. In short, Squirrely tells us he screwed up a gig that Barca paid him in advance for completion.

That kind of mistake means Barca owns Squirrely's ass.

"Look, man, all Barca wants is for us to shut down a particular power grid for six minutes during our hack. All we have to do is falsify an order from the Miami Attorney General and say it is a training exercise."

"I don't care what you call it," I counter. "This *training exercise* is not part of the hack."

And training is one thing we don't have enough time for in this smooth silo gig. Failure almost always thrives from a lack of practice. While he wasn't a Bushido warrior, I think it was the Greek poet Archilochus who said *we don't rise to the level of our expectations, we fall to the level of our training.*

What did the Greeks know, anyway? They only invented almost everything.

"Look, man, it's easy because Barca already sent me administrative access codes for this." Squirrel_Lord says as he hands me a piece of paper.

I immediately ball it up and throw it back at him. “Don’t muddy this water, Squirrely.”

My no is only temporary. Nobody should be owned by Barca. He collects hackers that owe him favors like children collect insects. Or cans. Or whatever children collect. I just need more time to process this idea of helping Barca before committing to it.

And, like Mane-Eac and I did yesterday, I need to plan a possible work-around should the stench of foul play get too strong for our delicate noses.

Something like this, Barca handing us this order on top of the impossible gig, could not be more suspect if it came in a cake with lit dynamite candles. I want to ask why this facility needs to be shut down, but anything dealing with Barca is a He-Needs-And-You-Don’t-Know capacity.

“We have to tell Ms. Magnolia,” I say.

“Naw, man, don’t do that. She’ll bail if she finds this out.”

“Well, you can eat a dead gopher’s dick as well, squirrel man,” says a voice with the sultriness of Jessica Rabbit delivering the snark of Jessica Walter.

Of course, I’d already met with Mane-Eac earlier and prepped her. I wanted her to have a way out beforehand. Her dirty history with Barca meant she never batted an oversized eyelash when I told her how complicated this gig had gotten.

“I don’t bail.” she says. “Bailing is what you do to water.”

“This boat has holes…” I counter.

“Wouldn’t you know it?” She hands me a black notebook. “I brought my caulking gun.”

Now, in the parking garage, a trio of hackers and the client have less than forty-eight hours to figure out a plan, get it in motion, and complete it before DoGoodR gets sentenced to life in prison.

I have done harder things in less time, I lie to myself.

Chapter Eleven

Contractors

That night, we start with Mane-Eac's notes and scrum this sucker on two giant white boards, taking turns writing ideas for our plan. On the lefthand side, we write our goal: keep a kid from life imprisonment. Then, under the goal, we list the objectives: get into the building, erase the files, shut down the power to that part of the grid, and crash the servers. Then, we each take ninety second sprints to jot down ideas on the righthand side.

After each round of sprints, we take anything that looks useful, move it to the right white board, erase the left one, and start again.

This technique works great for kids with ADHD, Type A personality software developers, or hackers that can't help but talk over each other.

Before a standard gig, I usually hit the scrum board about six times in order to get a decent plan together. However, with this crew, even after twenty passes, we have a bunch of gibberish. It's not that the plan won't work if the pieces fall into place. No, it is that there is something more, something in the unknowns that itches my neck while also tightening my sphincter.

Like a snowflake in a roaring furnace.

"This isn't working because we can't get past the freaking front gate," I say more to myself than anyone else. It's 3:32 AM and we've gotten nowhere. "Call it a night?"

"We dub thee *Sir Night.*" Mane-Eac takes our impromptu laser pointer, a detached car antenna, and taps me on each shoulder. "You're not seeing what I'm seeing."

I rub the pre-sleep crust from my heavy eyes. "Do you see the same board I do?"

"Nope." She pats me on the shoulder. "I'm seeing Atlanta."

At her words, the idea hits me like I just missed a step walking down the stairs.

"You brilliant and beautiful beast."

She curtsies demurely. "Thanks, bitch."

In Atlanta, we hacked the largest soda maker in the country because a competitor had a new product launch coming out. We knew the company's corporate protocol removed the option to bribe or blackmail an executive. For a soda maker, their personal security made the Secret Service look like the Silly Service. To get what we needed, we had to use one of the company's outside contractors.

Our current hack is a completely different monster, but the same pitchforks might work.

That, or we end up in federal custody.

Chapter Twelve

Jump

Security are the most important people to any government facility. They keep people out and secrets in and have access to the facility's most vulnerable areas. They aren't the way to break in, however. Most security officers and personnel are double, even triple checked. They are so squeaky clean that you could eat off them.

The second most important people, however, don't work for the government at all, yet they have the same access as security. They are temporary employees that are contracted for one job and one job only: custodial.

And they are this gig's glimmer of hope. Our job now is to figure out which company is scheduled to clean tomorrow.

After triple checking, Squirrel_Lord gives us the bad news.

"No one works tomorrow."

A smattering of various profanity bounces around the room.

"But..."

Someone once told me that everything you say before the word but is inconsequential, because everything after it punches you in the face.

"But what, Squirrely?" asks Michelle.

He glances at his watch, then back at his laptop, and then he repeats this motion, attempting to counter his disbelief.

"The next shift for today starts in three hours."

Michelle says, "That's too soon."

Why does it matter to her? She's not even going to be there.

"Do you have the roster of employees working?" I ask.

"Yep."

"Numbers?"

"Uno."

"Got a cell number?"

"Even better. Home address."

Mane-Eac and I exchange a glance. It is now or never. We can still pull out of this gig and avoid getting caught. But both of us believe in this cause because no one should have to spend his or her life in jail just because the government got lazy. This look is probably reserved for people who dive out of perfectly good airplanes for fun.

Like the band Van Halen said, *might as well jump*.

Chapter Thirteen

Strays

In the next hour, everyone gets their last phone calls in, just in case. Mane-Eac tackles some calls that only she and I know about. I don't trust Squirrel_Lord, and I trust Michelle even less. There's still time to cancel. If my gut is correct, doing so might end up with us in more trouble and less leverage to get out of it. If you're gonna break the law, it's best to shatter it.

Michelle calls someone, which is odd since she will not be on site. The client is never in harm's way. Maybe it is all above-board and she's just nervous.

While I don't question it, I make a mental note. Besides, her calling eases my mind a bit because, if Michelle is hiding something, then why make a phone call where any of us could eavesdrop?

I log into several bank accounts. Only one is mine, of course. Through a scrambled IP address, I make several transfers. All under the ten-thousand-dollar amount, so they will go through today, in case this plan goes ass-up. This is my backup plan, which I tell no one about. And, just like our current plan, it is half-baked.

I don't know who Squirrel_Lord calls, but I make one call about the only being that I can actually help at this point.

"Tropicana Animal Hospital. This is Tracy. How may I help you?"

"Yes, hi. This is Mr. Damascus. I was checking up on my pup."

I'm trying not to be a dog person. Dogs can slow you down and blow your cover in a dozen different ways. But I have a thing for strays.

Chapter Fourteen

Rancid and Sweet

Four Weeks Ago

I was completing a gig in Las Vegas. It was probably three, maybe four in the morning when I was walking to my Cash-Only hotel. I know better than to stay at an actual casino's hotel because there are more cameras in those places than in all of Hollywood. I was just about a block from Battista's Hole in the Wall, a fantastic restaurant that has stood the test of time as they have built casinos all around it, when a stack of cardboard boxes caught my attention. Someone did not set them out for recycling or garbage pick-up. Someone stacked them, and then tightly packed them together to form a protective cover from the weather.

Something in my gut drew me in. It was one of those feelings that was a warm feeling of protective confidence, and it told me to look inside the box. I stepped over empty Styrofoam boxes, plastic cups, and other discarded trash to get to the makeshift shelter. I guess the smell of car exhaust from vehicles whipping by masked the smell that ultimately flooded my nostrils when I got my face into the dark cover.

All I could see were the soles of shoes with holes in them and a blanket made of garbage bags covering the shelter's tenant. I'd smelled a dead body before, but this one was different. The Las Vegas heat had cooked the guy somehow, so the smell was equal parts rancid and sweet.

Then something moved under the tarp. Without thinking, I lifted the black plastic bags. From underneath, a skin-and-bones black Labrador retriever bounded my way. The dog immediately slammed into my chest, knocked me to the ground, and rolled over in submission.

I knew that there was a chance she got so hungry she fed off her former owner after he died. I covered my face with my hands, expecting to feel powerful canine teeth tearing into my protective hands.

Instead, I felt licks. I heard whimpers. And when I removed my hands, I looked up at the sweetest set of brown eyes I'd ever seen.

I backed up against a fence as my heart went from overdrive to merely speedy. Then, the poor dog took one step towards me, and collapsed. Then it tried again, with the same result. Again and again, until I got to her, picked her up, and carried her in my arms seven blocks to an all-night vet.

Chapter Fifteen

Hefty

I shake the memory away, as the front desk lady has already started answering my question.

"...Damascus. Thank you for checking in. She's doing really well, playing with the other big dogs. She's made a buddy with another Labrador, and they keep tugging over the same rope, but in a good way, not a possessive one, that is."

When I'd gotten her to the vet that first night in Vegas, she was down to thirty-two pounds. A dog that size is supposed to weigh around fifty-five. After learning I'd only just found her, the vet said he would keep her overnight for observation and start her on a diet designed for malnourished animals.

The vet said he would log her into the system as a stray. Something in my gut told me to ask him if he would record her as my dog. The Hispanic vet with oversized glasses lowered them and looked me up and down. After this ocular pat down, he told me that dogs that aren't strays need a name.

I told him her name was Hefty. He laughed, thinking I was making a play on her scrawny frame. I was actually referring to the brand of garbage bag I found her under.

Then he asked where I found her. At this, I had already planned my lie and told him I found her just a block from the vet's clinic. I knew that if the police found the dead man and the vet found out that she may have eaten some of him to survive, she would immediately get put down.

To me, she was a survivor. And, in my opinion, survivors shouldn't get put down for doing what they must do to survive.

Chapter Sixteen

Lucky Me

I clear my throat before getting back to asking the vet about my dog. “Is Hefty eating?” *Hopefully not people, that is…*

“Like a horse.”

In the background, a chorus of howls.

“Do you want to schedule a pickup for Hefty?”

“No, but I have a friend who will pick her up in a couple of days if you don’t hear from me.”

I’d already scheduled an email to go out to my lawyer if I didn’t log into my system within twenty-four hours.

“I may have to go out of town for work for an extended time, but my card on file should cover any expenses.”

“Lucky you! I love traveling!”

“Yeah,” I say, considering again the strong possibility of this hack going horribly wrong. “Lucky me.”

Chapter Seventeen

Burn

In the next hour, I do the traditional *death day* ritual: drop a sealed envelope to my lawyer in the blue mailbox on the corner. It contains keys to my apartment, a Do-Not-Resuscitate Living Will, and my actual Will (and where I've hidden my money).

I learned about *death day* from a guy in special operations with the U.S. Army, except his envelope included pictures of his wife and kids, as well as his obituary. I have none of the former and no one would care enough for me to write the latter.

Once my lawyer gets the envelope, he'll know to check all channels to see if I am dead or caught. The emergency email I have scheduled to go out will prep him, of course. There is just as good a chance of us getting shot-on-sight as there is getting caught-and-cuffed. His fee is in the envelope, too. A hacker named Alien taught me to never forget to pay the lawyer in advance, because the best-case scenario is you won't need him, and you bought goodwill.

It might be morbid, but it is reality.

Back inside the abandoned office building we're using for the night, our team of misfits stand in a circle. Sleep deprived and with half a plan, we sound off.

"Squirrely, do you have the abduction van?"

"Sí señor."

"Box cutters, lights, batteries, blankets, plus all our lock-picking gear?"

"In the duffel in said van, homey. We have enough gear in there to trigger a Stranger Danger Alert."

His poor attempt at humor gets met with a punch in the arm by Mane-Eac.

"Mane-Eac, do you have the knock-out gear?"

"Boom."

She extends her hands and shows the goodies: a taser with its charge setting glowing a fully-charged green in her left hand. In her right appears to be a standard blue-gray asthma inhaler. The cartridge is not something standard, like a pressurized prescription canister. Instead, the round metal canister looks more like a silver grape.

"What's with the inhaler?" asks Michelle.

"It contains a specialized knockout gas. Actual ingredients are above my IQ. It takes a while to work. You wouldn't know it from watching movies, but anything that works in just a matter of seconds causes brain damage. We only want the guard temporarily incapacitated. The taser takes him down. The tranq takes him out."

"Oh, good," says Michelle, her voice cracking, clearly concerned we were going to kill someone on this hack.

There are certain lines even I will never cross.

"Michelle, we will meet you at the rendezvous point after we finish."

"I'm going with you."

This is not part of the plan.

"Michelle, if we get caught..."

"I'm willing to risk it. Look, everyone here is trying to help DJ. And so am I."

"Girlie, please." Squirrel_Lord chuckles. "Why don't you just tell them?"

Squirrely breaks the circle and crosses over to Michelle. He towers over her, and a smile worthy of a cartoon villain crosses his lips. The look on her face is equal parts panic and fear.

What does Squirrel_Lord know?

"You're a thrill-chaser, ain't cha?" He beats on his chest, our emo gorilla on the hunt. "Me too!"

"Cut the crap." Michelle shoves him aside and darts over to Mane-Eac and me. "I'll be a lookout if the three of you are running code. Besides, with a plan held together by thin spiderwebs, the more people that are there, the better."

As much as I distrust her, Michelle makes a decent point. Our cup runneth over with unknowns.

"Fine," I say, "but the moment this spinning top wobbles, you bail. None of our planned escape route guarantees your safety, do you understand?"

"Yes."

I put my hand out. Mane-Eac puts her gold leather gloved one on mine. Michelle adds hers. Finally, Squirrel_Lord's black painted nails land on top. We pump once and release.

"Alright," I say, and open the door. "Let's burn this sucker down."

Chapter Eighteen

Bumper Cars

A problem with plans is that they function like babies on the set of a movie: the director hopes they will remain quiet during the shot, but there is a greater chance they will throw a shit-fit and ruin everything.

That's what happens when we arrive at the home of the custodian.

"Shit," says Michelle. "His car is gone."

"I thought Mane, er, Ms. Magnolia said he wouldn't be leaving for work yet."

"Well, thanks for singling me out, squirrel man," says Mane-Eac as she flips through a yellow legal pad. "So, you don't see his Tercel?"

"Wait," I say. "Didn't we pass one on the way here?"

"Then go, go, go!" yells Mane-Eac.

I pull a U-turn and gun the engine.

"Head towards the worksite."

As we make a left and head towards the highway, I check my watch: eight fifty-five. Without announcing it, I veer off on a frontage road and head down a two-lane street.

"What are you doing?" asks Michelle. "The worksite is that way."

"Technically, yes," I answer. "However, he's probably avoiding the highway congestion. If he stays on the highway, he'll hit nine o'clock traffic. My gut says he's hitting the frontage road adjacent to avoid a traffic jam."

Michelle asks, "How in the hell do you know that?"

"Because it is what I would do."

Sure enough, after three blocks, a rusty maroon color early 90s Tercel is in front of us.

"Tag confirmation?" I ask Mane-Eac.

"It's him," she answers.

"Awesome." I swallow hard, but my saliva works against me and lumps in my throat, choking me. "N-n-ow for the bad part."

Forty yards away, I spot an empty parking lot in front of an abandoned building. I slam on the gas. Our van bashes into the Tercel's bumper, knocking it clear off the car. As the car pulls off to the side of the road, Mane-Eac rolls down her window.

"What the ever-loving hell, lady?" yells a guy in a stereotypical Brooklyn accent. "Who taught ya friend how to drive?"

"I am so, so, so sorry! It is my fault. I was complaining to him about how he shouldn't drive like a race car driver. The next thing you know, he hits you. So sorry!"

"My bad." I lean across towards the window. "So, we're just gonna go now."

"The hell you are!" The man's cheeks flush and he hits the steering wheel with his fists. "I'm gonna be late because of yous! You betta have good insurance, pal!"

"Damnation, man," I say and point towards the parking lot. "Look, I'll pull over there and we can get our stuff sorted out."

"Fine," mumbles the man. "I'll sort you out…"

I pull into the lot at an angle that puts the driver's side of the car facing the abandoned building's wall. Our New Yorker parks his car a few yards away. He exits his car, walks to the back of his car, and puts his hands on his head in disgust. "Oh, you've gotta be kidding me!"

"Things happen." I raise my hands palms up. "Life is like a game of bumper cars."

"Why you little…"

When the custodian reaches through the driver's side window and grabs my shirt, I zap him with the handheld taser. An electric crackling emits from it as well as the faint smell of ozone, almost like chlorine from a swimming pool, as the guy falls to the ground. As he shakes, Mane-Eac darts out of the van and straddles his chest. Squirrel_Lord and I hold down one arm and leg each on the man. Mane-Eac shoves the inhaler in his mouth with one hand and closes his nose with the other. One pump later, he coughs and struggles to get up.

"Letta go of me, you…wait…what did you…"

"Shh…" Mane-Eac strokes his hair and holds his head. "It's sleepy baby time…"

The man struggles, kicks, bites, and yells for a good minute or so until…

"What…now you just…you just…you…"

The man's eyes roll back in his head. Mane-Eac cradles his unconscious skull and keeps it from striking the concrete. Then she rises from her spot on his chest, and spins around to lift him from his armpits. Squirrel_Lord and I each grab a leg, and together, we carry the guy into the van through the open side sliding door.

Squirrel_Lord wheezes and wipes sweat from his brow. "Man, he's heavier than he looks."

"That's funny," counters Mane-Eac, "because you're just as dumb as you look."

"You two cut it out and roll him over."

Once the man is on his back, we go through his pockets, getting his car keys and his ID card.

"Okay, I'll drive the custodian's car to a block away from the worksite. Everyone else, follow in the van. Once there, we will all load up."

Michelle glances around the vehicle. "Won't the security guard notice three extra people when only one is supposed to show up?"

I reach into the duffel bag that Squirrel_Lord put in earlier and pull out one of the four box-cutters. I roll its triangular blade out, then slide it back in.

"Oh, so you're going to take the guard hostage?"

"Nothing like that," I say, handing out the boxcutters. I point at Michelle with one. "Please be a dear and grab that broken bumper in the street."

Chapter Nineteen

Tools

Every smuggler out there knows that the average car seat has over two feet of padding in it. Michelle, with her Olympic gymnast build, fits perfectly in there. It is uncomfortable, but we are only going a few blocks.

Now, a back seat, bench style, has closer to three feet of padding, which is why Squirrel_Lord and Mane-Eac are head-to-toe packed together like sardines in a can in that one. I'm sure both will make jokes when we finish this about getting stuck in the worst sixty-nine experience of his or her life.

Anything more than a cursory glance will reveal smuggled humans in this vehicle. Luckily, since I knocked the bumper off this car, I have it laying at an angle from the front passenger seat to the back driver's side.

As I approach the security officer's post, I put the car in the park gear and roll down my window.

"Morning."

"Morning," responds the guy in the black hat and jacket that both read Security. He never glances up from his newspaper as he extends his right.

I shake it.

This is the wrong move, because the security guard instantly brings his focus to me. His eyes go from glazed over to pinpointed on my face.

"No, I need your ID..."

"Oh, right." *Stupid Tanto*. I hand him a forged one, a Radio Frequency Identification card that has my picture, and copied RFID information on it from the security guard. Hopefully, it will be enough to clear me.

The guard slides the card through the reader. A red light turns green, and the gate in front of the car opens. The guard hands back the card and waves me through.

I shift gears from Park to Drive. Just as I do this, the guard yells out, "Hold up!"

Shit.

"Put it in Park!"

I put the car back in Park and lean out the window. Maybe I can talk my way out of this.

"Sir, I—"

"Sit back," commands the guard, his flat tone striking my nerves with pinpoint accuracy.

I sit back. The guard leans in and looks over the vehicle as I try to control my nervous hands by gripping the steering wheel as hard as I can. Then the guard leans back and walks behind the car. He does a full circle around the vehicle.

What is he thinking?

The guard winds up in front of our car. He taps the car's hood as his eyes lock on me.

Something is up. Throw it into Reverse and gun it out of here.

The guard moves his hand towards his holstered revolver.

I could hit the gas. I could run this man over. We could get away.

But that would kill him. And I do not kill.

Instead, I wave both my hands at him. He does not even raise an eyebrow.

The guard walks towards my window and moves his hand from his revolver to his back pocket. Once he arrives at my window, he pulls out his wallet and hands me a business card from it.

"Look man, my brother-in-law is an auto mechanic. Here's his card. Just tell him Andrew sent you."

"Ah, thanks, man!" I manage to squeak out, taking the card from him.

"Alright, you have a good day."

"You too, sir."

As I drive us up to the side of the building and park us in one of the farthest spots behind the building and out of view of the security guard, only then do I take a breath. In front of us are two doors: one big and one small. To the side of the building is an old, rusted RV surrounded by a gravel patch. The rust and busted windows on it show it has seen better days.

From the literal passenger seat, I hear, “Well, that went well.”

“Speak for yourself,” counters Mane-Eac. “You didn’t have a sweaty reject roadie from The Cure squirming all over you.”

“Well, I love *The Cure*. Thank you for the compliment, you little bit-ow-that’s-a-ball-that’s-a-ball-ow.”

I exit the vehicle and yank the covers off *Bonnie and Snide* in the backseat first. This plan is tough enough as it is without Mane-Eac castrating Squirrel_Lord. We’ll save that joy for another day.

After I cut Michelle out of her chair, I scan the exterior. The servers’ building is nothing exceptional: a gray concrete building with a bunch of external air conditioners lining the outside perimeter. That makes sense: these servers put off a lot of heat.

If we were only here to destroy the servers, all we would need to do is cut off the AC, overclock the furnaces, and let the computers cook themselves.

The plan we have in mind needs much more handholding. First, we must get past those motion-sensitive cameras. It is not a problem if the camera sees little-old-me, but multiple people entering the building could be a huge problem.

You can tell the difference between always-recording and motion-sensitive equipment by the small boxes next to the camera. If a camera has a lit red bulb, it is always recording. If it has a square box that looks like a barcode scanner in a grocery store check-out line that is near an unlit red bulb, it is motion sensitive.

What most people don’t know about these cameras is that they dislike light of any kind. Light overwhelms them. That is why most footage you see on police TV shows has grainy day recordings, yet the night vision footage is crystal-clear.

I motion to Squirrel_Lord. He drops the duffel bag on the ground from his shoulder. It crashes to the ground, and sound like glass breaking hits my ears.

"I swear if that came from the bag..." Then I answer my own inquiry: someone broke beer bottles and left them strewn across the gravel. *Phew.*

From the duffel, I pull out three FlashTorches. I've kept these flashlight-like prototypes in my bug-out bag for just the right occasion. Unfortunately, I brought no batteries, which is why I asked Squirrel_Lord to grab them before breakfast.

What is so cool about these *Star Wars* lightsaber looking things is that they send out light so powerful that, if you put your hand in front of a beam for any length of time, you'll wind up with a sunburn. Any longer exposure can ignite a wet-wood campfire, which is why wilderness campers will love these things when they hit the market.

In theory, these beams will not only prevent the system from alarming security about our trespassing, but also fry the motion-sensitive circuits in those cameras.

In theory. I've never tested this idea before, but beggars on a limited timetable can't be choosers.

I point out to the team the three cameras that might track us, although the one in the far-left corner does not appear to be pointed our way. Its angle is more towards the side of the building but, depending on the type of lens in the camera's housing, it could still track our movements.

Mane-Eac and Squirrel_Lord each take the closest cameras to our point of entry. I focus on our distant sensor.

"Okay, we go on my mark in one-second step patterns with each step no longer than a foot in length," I say as everyone nods. "According to a buddy of mine that works on motion detector software, collective movements have less of a chance of activating the recording protocol than ungrouped ones."

"Squirrely, you got the goods?"

He adjusts the duffel bag's strap on his shoulder and sends me a wink.

"Go."

The crunch of gravel under our feet assists our march. These steps make us sound like we're going to storm a castle. Maybe that's my Bushido mindset doing what it does: filtering the world in an ancient, yet logical way.

We actually make it to within ten steps of the door before this plan does what most plans do: go awry.

"Um, I've got a situation here," says Mane-Eac through gritted teeth. The sound of her golden gloved hand smacking the side of the flashlight tells me everything I need to know.

I ask a dumb question to which my gut already knows the dumb answer. "Squirrely, did you put new batteries in these damn things?"

"Um…new-ish. I just took the batteries out of a couple of remote controls. They were working fine before!"

"For that low level of draw, yes, but not intense light, moron!"

In seconds, we're as exposed as a nudist in church.

I keep my beam on and move it a few feet from my target in the distance. As I do, a red-light flicks on. I immediately return my beam to the sensor.

Shit. I'm still too far away to short out the sensor.

Several steps away, I spot the edge of a metal drain gutter that might block that camera's view of us. But that's a risk. There is a chance that Mane-Eac's beam has burned out her sensor, but there's no way to know for sure.

"Michelle, run to the door," I command. "Ms. Magnolia, I am about to shift my light to your—"

"Move!" she yells.

As Mane-Eac's beam dies, the red light on the top of her camera flickers.

"Run!" screams Squirrel_Lord, dropping his beam from its target. Its red bulb, too, flashes.

My sneakers peel out on the gravel, making me look like a real-life cartoon character revving up to run, throwing me off balance. As my left hand smacks the ground, giving me a bit of traction, I sprint with all the agility my tiny legs can give me towards the door.

Michelle is already there. She's waving us in like we're swimming in the ocean, and she's just spotted a shark fin near us. Just like in that situation, waving doesn't do a damn bit of good.

My heart pounds as I realize I am at least four strides from the door. Both cameras' red lights flicker.

Mane-Eac dives under the awning and out of the cameras' views.

Three strides to go.

Squirrel_Lord passes me like I am standing still. *Curse him and his long legs.*

Two strides.

In the distance, a siren blares. Squirrely turns towards the sound. He slips on loose gravel and tumbles to the ground.

The flickering lights now pump a bright, solid red. Someone or something now watches our every move.

As the siren continues, I stop to grab Squirrel_Lord, but my feet slip on the loose rocks. I land on my left leg, and it slams right into a broken beer bottle. Searing pain shoots up my leg and I scream at not just one, but two pieces lodged in my leg. I yank out one of the amber glass pieces. My jeans instantly go from blue to red. It's not a deep gash, but it still hurts like hell.

However, the second one comes out with minimal pain. An icy chill of fear runs down my spine and I shove my left hand under Squirrely's collar. My other hand slides under his belt buckle. With adrenaline and pure stubbornness, I squat and yank the string bean looking Goth to his black booted feet.

Together, we stumble under the awning and collapse on the concrete floor in front of the door. Once everyone is together, we all gasp for air while tensely waiting for police.

This plan might shift from a break-in plan to a spread-out-and-scatter panic.

Then, the siren stops. After a full minute, no more sirens roar. No police cars arrive. Not even the security guard moseys over to see what the fuss is all about.

We just got away with what is probably the easiest part of this damn plan.

I am still face-down on the concrete in a small puddle of my own drool that's collected while I was trying not to have a heart attack.

Mane-Eac stands up, dusts her leather pants off, and sends out the circular hand signal for okay to me. I send one back. As for Squirrel_Lord, she flips him the bird and turns her head instead of waiting for a response.

I roll up to a seated position just as Michelle asks through catchy breathing a question to which I, unfortunately, already know the horrible answer.

"Where...where...where's the...duffel?"

There, in the distance, where I stopped to pick up Squirrel_Lord, is the duffel bag with all the tools we need to get into the steel front door.

Chapter Twenty

And like that...

For the next three minutes, Squirrel_Lord and I take turns giving everyone worse and worse news. I withdraw the security guard's RFID card in my jean pocket and, before I even look at it, my heart knows that my fall on broken glass did more than just slice my leg.

In the card is a gash. As I examine the damage, it is apparent that my fall punctured its magnetic strip, the part with our door access code. Even so, we try to use it to open the door.

After four different error lights flash on the pad, our crew understands what needs to happen, even though no one says it out loud.

We're going to have to break in the old-fashioned way.

To the side of the human-sized door is another larger one. It is probably what they use for moving in larger machinery. Unfortunately, both doors are thick steel, in that every time we tap on it in various places, we hear no echo. If one section would just ting from our taps a little, it would provide a sliver of hope.

It is not like we have any tools to cut through it with us. The big door's lock is military grade, meaning that, even if we MacGyver'd some lock picking tools from hairpins, paperclips, or random debris, we still couldn't break enough pins in the lock to get through. A professional locksmith would have to drill through these locks. Even that might backfire. Both doors feature recessed hinges, so there's no knocking them off their braces. And there's not even any gap between the doors' bases and the floor, which means we can't angle something up from under them and grab a doorknob.

We might not get in if we had our tools. They designed the lock pick kit in the duffel for cabinets, drawers, and less secure doors, like ones you would find entering a bathroom. As it is, we only have a clear paper bag with someone's discarded fast food lunch that Michelle found in the corner with an empty hamburger wrapper, five fries, and a medium soda fountain cup. Mane-Eac's using the cup like she's in a spy movie; the wide end is against the stucco wall and the smaller end is against her ear.

"Did you check under the mat?" asks Michelle as she points at the faded rubber doormat that reads *All Work and No Play Makes Jack a Rich Boy*.

Part of me wants to counter Michelle's comment because I don't think someone is stupid enough to hide keys to a government server room under a mat anymore. A larger part of me lifts and looks because I trust humanity so little that I look both ways when entering a One-Way Street. Unfortunately, I only find two cockroaches that do what I should've done the moment Squirrel_Lord approached me with this gig: flee.

"We're not getting in?" asks Michelle.

I shake my head as I stare into the door lock like my mind will unlock it or something.

"We were so close, man," mutters Squirrel_Lord as he slumps down next to me.

"Maybe if someone hadn't cheaped-out and gotten us used batteries, we would be inside by now." Sure, my tone is one of righteous accusation, and stating the obvious never helps cut the tension from a situation, but I'm more than pissed. I'm drained.

"Hey, I only did that for one flashlight..."

I point to the duffel bag in the distance. "Case in point."

"You're a rotten son of bitch, do you know that?"

"Spot on," I say, "but you're still an idiot."

Through all our bickering, Mane-Eac scoots both of us to the right side of the smaller door and yanks up the door mat.

"Hey, I already checked for a key, Ms. Magnolia," I snap at her.

"You men lay there and cry," she replies, unbothered, "and let me do my thing."

Squirrel_Lord extends his black nail-polished fingernails towards the yard. "Why don't we just go out there and get our tools?"

"Because we only have one light and they have three working cameras, moron."

"Well, how do we even get out of here?"

"I don't know, okay?" I pull at my dirty blonde hair. "It wasn't supposed to go like this."

"Well, how was it supposed to, *Mr. Marigold*?"

Somehow, his sarcastic tone, accompanying my fake handle, drives my sanity off a cliff. I slap the ever-loving shit out of Squirrel_Lord. Then he throws a punch my way, which I see coming, and duck my head. His right fist pops as he punches me in the forehead, which hurts his hand more than it hurts me. Granted, my head now throbs like someone is throwing an impromptu disco in my skull.

The next thing I know, we are rolling around on the ground and wrestling like a couple of kindergarteners: getting more winded than causing any damage.

"If you don't cut this out, I'll put you both in the corner." Mane-Eac drives her fingernails into both of our necks, and we break loose from each other. Without missing a beat, she hands one end of the rubber doormat to me and the other to Squirrel_Lord.

"What do you say you two become useful and hold that mat right here?" The stern look in her eyes reminds me of a schoolteacher I had when I was around ten: beady, with the ability to melt ice.

Neither Squirrely nor I argue as we stand and hold the mat against the stucco wall. At first, I think Mane-Eac kicking her black and yellow steel toed Caterpillar boot into the mat is in response to our pointless bickering. After the third kick, I notice the fist-sized hole that her size six boot has made in the wall.

Six kicks later, Mane-Eac shoves the mat aside from the hole. Dust and bits of plaster fill the air as she glances in the hole. Mane-Eac extends her left arm back toward me.

"Give me the mat."

I hand it to her, and she shoves it into the hole. "Do you want to let the rest of the class know what you're doing?"

"Class is for rich folks." Mane-Eac squints and adjusts the mat. "But you're welcome to think for yourself."

Do you know that idiotic feeling you get when you ask someone where the ketchup is in the fridge and then someone points right at it like it wasn't hiding from your view the whole time? That's what happens when I glance in this hole just to the right of the armored door's doorknob as Mane-Eac steps away.

Wiring. Not alarm system grade, or server grade. Not that thick and multicolored type. Electrical. The thin kind that connects light switches to electrical current. That's why Mane-Eac used the rubber doormat when she kicked. She needed to make a hole, but also didn't want to get electrocuted.

The combination of a steel-toed boot and doormat is the lock pick set we didn't ask for but sure as hell needed.

Through the hole, there's a light switch immediately next to the doorknob, just like in every home in America. That's why this area isn't shielded by metal, like the door and walls are. Someone installed the lights after they built the walls, but prior to their reinforcement.

Also, keeping metal away from those wires keeps from having a large conduit, like steel, that might lead to a fire.

God bless the Fire Marshall.

That reminds me to look for a fire alarm system when I get inside.

"You are one brilliant babe, Ms. Magnolia."

"Mr. Marigold, do you want to do the honors?"

"How about we let Squirrely use those long limbs and fingers for once?" I move away as Squirrel_Lord wraps the wires in the rubber mat and pushes his hand through the interior's drywall. Once through, he leans elbow deep into the wall and reaches up.

While biting his tongue, Squirrel_Lord unlocks the top lock, then the bottom.

And like that, we're in.

W. A. Pepper

Chapter Twenty-One

Flush

In the movies, server rooms are vast, yet orderly, rows of monitorless workstations with flickering blue and red lights. These shiny and beautiful machines produce a light hum and have hidden keyboards and monitors that slide out easily and then instantly boot up, right to the screen where the hackers need to go. I even think I saw one movie where the director used the Star Trek smooth whoosh sound of doors opening for the keyboard sliding out from its recessed shelf.

In reality, the United States of America's government outsources everything to the lowest bidder. That's why, once we all step inside the backup server room, the team surveys this fuster-cluck of a technology wasteland.

"This looks like a defunct junior college's *Computers for Crackheads* classroom." Several coughs leave my chest because of the hot and dusty air. After I turn on a series of flickering fluorescent bulbs, we get a better view of the sadness: strewn throughout the room are piecemealed servers. They produce a high-pitched whine that clicks off right before they reach a migraine-inducing level of screeching.

"Damnation," says Squirrel_Lord. "These machines are asking for the release of sweet death."

"There are more wires strung across this room than Spider-Man's wet dream," Mane-Eac adds.

"Well, that should make the erasing of the hard drives a cakewalk, but this old tech is gonna screw with our access to the onsite servers." I reach into my pocket and withdraw a Pez dispenser featuring bald-headed Charlie Brown from the cartoon strip Peanuts. "Adderall anyone?"

"Don't mind if I do." Mane-Eac says, snatching one from Charlie's plastic throat and dry swallowing it. Squirrel_Lord and I do the same. While it'll take roughly twenty minutes to kick in, and snorting would be quicker, I don't see anywhere clean to crush it up. Better to wait for digestion than inhale some asbestos or something.

It also helps that the Pez dispenser has a hidden thumb drive in its bottom with keystroke recording software on it.

I extend the Pez dispenser to Michelle. She waves me away. I guess drugs aren't her thing. I usually don't do this kinda stuff outside of hacking. But, then again, I'm almost always hacking, so I'm on this or the harder stuff. As Hank Williams, Jr. sang, my drug intake is *a family tradition.*

Both Mane-Eac and Squirrel_Lord take seats in front of keyboards and ancient monitors, the kind that take a full minute to boot up. I explore the room before heading to a closed door in the back.

"What are you looking for?" asks Michelle. Her tone is flat, almost bored. Maybe she doesn't realize that a huge part of hacking is understanding the tools you have before you start.

After a few tugs, I pry open the plain, white door with the rusty doorknob.

"I'm looking for where someone wrote a password." Inside the room, I find the phone line going out connected to a red box with a flame on it. "And I've found jack squat."

"What, do you expect it to be that easy?" she asks with a snicker. This tells me she has more faith in humanity's intelligence than I do.

I grab the red cable attached to the red box. However, I'm not looking at the cable itself: in my hand is a burner phone, complete with a black cable, AKA a dongle, hanging from its end.

On the phone, there are no reception bars. This place isn't too far from any cell towers. I even saw one about half a mile away from the security gate when we entered.

No, someone set this place up like the Faraday bag I used to shut off any signals from our cellphones at the gig's first meeting. This place is locked down. There is no cell signal in or out.

"Hey, Ms. Magnolia, did you get a Charlie?" No one calls Adderall a Charlie. This code will tell Mane-Eac exactly what to do next: wait for my signal, then scan the perimeter. She takes the hint and Mane-Eac distracts Michelle by asking her to look at something on her screen. I use this opportunity to unhook the landline from the fire alarm and hook it to my cellphone. If this gig eventually goes FUBAR, then just the appearance of this little phone and its funky cable hooked up to a way to contact the outside world might save our asses.

Back when this gig started, I used the Faraday bag for more than just signal blocking. It is an example of control. Without control, or at least perceived control, there is the risk of exposure. And exposure infects everything with unknowns.

As I turn back, I catch Michelle staring at me.

How much did she see, and does her seeing me actually hurt the plan?

I move forward with the backup plan and withdraw the Pez dispenser from my right pocket.

Mane-Eac extends her hand in the air. "I'm developing a tolerance, so let me hold on to the candy," she says.

I underhandedly toss it to her, but it falls to the ground near a workstation.

"You throw like a child."

"Sorry I'm not into sportsball, Ms. Magnolia."

She mutters something under her breath as she kneels to where the Pez dispenser fell.

I join the work by grabbing a seat. Michelle walks around and supervises, which is more than a little irritating.

You're our client, not our babysitter.

After about half an hour, the work becomes automatic. These machines already have access to the onsite servers that they are supposed to back up, though the limited, initial connection takes three straight hours of penetration testing – or pentests – of the security firewalls before Mane-Eac finally breaks through them.

"And that's how the sausage is made," she says, pleased with herself.

A siren goes off in my brain. She's always been a talented data miner, gathering hidden nuggets from servers, but Squirrel_Lord is definitely better at Dam Breaking, or breaking firewalls. His failure to get through sits uncomfortably in my gut.

For the next five minutes, I pace as Mane-Eac bounces from server to server as Michelle and Squirrel_Lord observe. One server contains personnel records of all U.S. Attorney employees. Another contains all the inside memos from staff. Finally, she finds one that catalogs and holds all evidence. Such as DJ's.

"Great work, Ms. Magnolia," I say. "I'll trade out with you."

"The *E* key sticks on here." Her hands fly across the keyboard as she stands. "But if you want the honors, I'm game."

I bump into Mane-Eac as she stands. The computer's mouse, a grayish wired one with yellow stains on it from years of human sweat, smacks to the floor next to the base of the computer.

"Shit, my bad."

"You're as graceful as a tap-dancing hippo, Mr. Marigold." Mane-Eac kneels and retrieves the mouse for me. "Here you go, clumsy. I'm off for a smoke break."

This *smoke break* might reveal my darkest fears.

"Wait," interrupts Michelle. "Don't you want to watch?"

"Girl, it ain't a magic trick," Mane-Eac chuckles. "Besides, I'll be back by the time he finishes up."

"Enjoy your cancer stick, Ms. Magnolia." I fire finger pistols at her. "I'm sure one of these windows opens up."

As Mane-Eac strolls off and opens the closest window, I look through all the onsite server directories. From inside of the personnel directory, I create an administrative account and create the falsified reboot work order that Barca required of Squirrel_Lord and send it off.

"Oh, shit." I hit the *Escape* key, but nothing happens.

"What?" asks Squirrel_Lord.

"I totally forgot to include the Administrative codes that Barca gave you before I hit Send…"

Except I didn't. I'm playing a hunch.

"Um, well, um, oh no!"

Squirrely's acting needs some workshopping.

"Well, Squirrel_Lord, knowing the GSA or 'Go Slow Administration,' this might get through in six to nine weeks," I say.

A rusty creak echoes throughout the room as Mane-Eac opens another window.

"Can't you just pick a window already?" snaps Squirrel_Lord, digging into his ear canal with his pinky finger.

"The wind keeps blowing smoke in my face," she answers.

Then, my fake email account dings. I open it.

"Order received. Shutting sector down now."

"Holy shit, um, that's, um, that's great…"

Squirrel_Lord's lack of enthusiasm about getting what he wanted, as well as the speed at which this order comes through, confirms two sneaking suspicions I've had since he came to me with this gig.

There is no need for any administrative code, and this hack has zero to do with the monster known as Barca.

I glance over at Mane-Eac, who's on her third window. She knocks the ashes from the cigarette before snuffing it out on the window seal and grinding the tobacco way past the point of extinguishing a flame.

She glances my way and nods. My stomach turns sour.

Too late to turn back now.

Just for good measure, I hit a few more keystrokes. None of them matter. I even intentionally mistype a few commands to buy Mane-Eac time as she heads to the bathroom in the back. I haven't accidentally missed a keystroke since I was learning how to type using the DOS *Wizard of Id* typing game and still young enough to order the McDonald's happy meal.

What an odd time to think about that game.

Maybe that's how my brain is coping with the guillotine that hovers by a thread above our necks.

"Wait," says Squirrel_Lord, as he approaches Mane-Eac. "Come watch."

"I told you I'm good, so I'll just hit the headfirst."

"It'll only take a second."

He puts his arm under hers and basically carries her over. Any other time, she'd break free. We can't risk letting anyone know what we know, so she reluctantly joins us instead of going to the restroom. Once there, she yanks her arm out of his grasp.

I pull up the screen to wipe the data on both the onsite servers and in this room. Then I stand up from the keyboard and motion for Michelle to sit.

"Michelle, would you like to do the honors?"

"Look, you've done amazing work. This is all yours."

"Hey, it's your boyfriend," says Mane-Eac. "If it were my partner, I'd gladly do the honors."

"No, I'm good."

With Squirrel_Lord and Michelle's full attention on me and the station, Mane-Eac quietly steps backwards.

"Okay, then Squirrely," I say, stepping to him, "I hate that you got left out of actually doing some of the work, so all you have to do is hit *Enter*."

"Man, T, er Mr. Marigold, you two did all the work, so it is your honor."

I almost laugh at the perfect, intentional phrasing: *You two did all the work.*

I glance around the ceiling. There are six smoke detectors in this room. Four look especially worn. *I wonder if those are the mic'd ones.*

"Honor." I mumble the word. These two know nothing of the word, especially Squirrel_Lord. He has lowered himself below even a hacker's code, one of payment for a job, and much less the Bushido one.

I think back to Hefty, how she did what was necessary to survive. Knowing that, there's a part of me that can't blame Squirrel_Lord for this betrayal.

Of course, that part is about the size of a grain of sand, but it exists.

When the motion sensor cameras didn't alert anyone, I should've known this was a trap.

"I tell you what Squirrely, you just put your finger on the *Enter* key, and I'll press it. What do you say?"

A bead of sweat drips down his face. His lips smack because his mouth is drying. Over Squirrel_Lord's shoulder, Mane-Eac gets smaller, slipping into the background.

"Man, naw, you, you can do it…"

So, this is how it goes down then.

I bow up as much as my five-eight frame allows and get even closer to the tall man. Now I am under Squirrely's face. His breath reeks of bile and deception.

He knows I know.

"Squirrel_Lord, touch the keyboard."

He closes his eyes. The soles of his boots on the concrete floor squeak like a small mouse in the corner as he shifts from foot to foot.

"Please, man, just press it, T."

The word *press* strings across the room on an invisible rope, almost daring someone to pluck it from the air. Squirrel_Lord's breathing shifts from deep breaths to shallow ones, tiny sips of air. If this were a spaghetti western type movie from the 1960s or 1970s, there would be a whistle in the background of this standoff.

I draw first.

"Now!" I yell.

Mane-Eac sprints to the back of the room.

"Targets are aware!" Michelle screams from behind Squirrel_Lord. "Move in! Repeat! Move in!" She reaches under a desk and pulls out a hidden, standard-issue 9mm Glock.

I shove Squirrel_Lord into her and the pair tumble to the ground.

Both the front and back doors of the building blast open. Soldiers in full SWAT attire storm in.

"Get on the ground!" a man yells through his mask.

Though it would be the wisest choice, it is the last thing I'll do.

As I run, I guess two things about these armed men. One, they won't shoot an unarmed man who is running away from them because forensics will show an entry wound in the back. And two, they're probably confused that I'm not running towards the exit.

I'm running toward the closed bathroom door.

The problem is, I'm about to be *armed*. When we first came in, I'd noticed a screwdriver with a tip the size of a piece of rice that someone left on the desk near the fire alarm system. The moment I touch it, they might shoot me.

I must risk it because I have to buy Mane-Eac time.

As I pick up the screwdriver mid-sprint, someone yells, "Suspect is armed!"

Before I know it, thunder hits my ears as two computer monitors behind me explode from shotgun fire. Even at this distance, the smell of gunpowder floods my nostrils as buckshot whizzes over my shoulder, the mere force of it whipping my clothing.

As I slam into the closed door, my heart echoes into my throat. My ears strain to hear the toilet flushing over the rush of blood to my head.

I shove the screwdriver's head into the doorknob's lock and break off its tip. This won't save Mane-Eac, but I'm not trying to give her time to get away. There might not be even any windows in the bathroom.

I'm not even trying to buy her minutes.

We only need seconds for this to work.

If it works.

A taser hits my back. A ticking of electricity fills my brain. My body twitches and bounces like a Mexican jumping bean.

A soldier attempts to turn the doorknob. Thankfully, even in this outdated building, old locks still work.

"We're…out of time…hurry!" I yell through the tremors. A gloved hand covers my mouth and the taste of leather and sweat hits my tongue.

A soldier shines his flashlight into the lock.

"Can't pick it." He points to a man near the front entrance with a handheld battering ram. "Break it down."

My every nerve holds for the sound of another flush. Mane-Eac has had time for the first flush, but that won't save us. One flush does nothing when you are getting rid of contraband. The first flush only shoves the evidence into the tank's reserve pipe. We need two flushes. I just hope the reservoir fills fast enough to give us a fighting chance of not winding up in jail for the rest of our lives.

The soldier with the battering ram squares up to the door. He pulls back the flat black rod and uses its weight and momentum to slam into the door. A loud crack echoes throughout the computer room.

The door hangs on by its hinges. It won't survive the next hit.

As the battering ram shatters the remaining parts of the door, the most joyful noise I can imagine occurs.

A second toilet flush.

Chapter Twenty-Two

Never. Say. You. Did. Nothing.

For the next hour, I kneel on bare concrete with my zip-tied hands and sweat, causing my back to itch incessantly. My knees have shifted from stabbing needle pains to flat-out numbness. My nose also itches, but I can't reach it, so I just wiggle it as much as I can. The inside of the black hood on my face smells like body odor, but also something sweet is there. *Ah. Cinnamon.* The last lucky fellow in this hood must've been chewing gum before getting hauled away. *I guess that is some sort of silver lining.*

The clickity-clacks of a keyboard tell me that this federal agency's tech guy is confirming everything we *attempted* to do. I use the word *attempted* because I knew hitting the *Enter* key was the final nail in the coffin for this sting. Hitting *Enter* would have added a lot of unwanted charges. Everything we did up to that point was conspiracy, intent, and trespassing, and those charges alone are enough to jail us for decades.

"How're you holding up?" I ask.

"Oh, I'm dandy," responds Mane-Eac. "I just willingly went into a Federal trap that you and I both knew, deep down, couldn't be more obvious if they put a big sign out front that read *Not a Trap, Come On In!*"

"I told you you didn't have to do this."

"And I told you I did."

I say, "Yet you never told me why."

The clickity-clacks fill the silence until Mane-Eac speaks again.

"Because of what you did for me during the Epic_Chaos fiasco."

"Oh, I didn't—"

"Never. Say. You. Did. Nothing."

Chapter Twenty-Three

Iguana

Years Ago

Mane-Eac's second gig with me was for a client neither of us had met before, a hacker handled Epic_Chaos. He was the type of preppy that was from Upstate New York, not New York, damn it. He was one of those school-taught hackers that the rest of us in the hacking community tolerate. These guys tend to hide behind theory and hypothetical hacks of what one could do if they used a particular set of tools. The rest of us self-taught hackers got our callouses by trial and error. Actually, more like trial and judicial sentencing, because we took actual risks.

This six-foot-two dude, with bleached blond hair and teeth so white and shiny he could sell real estate with a smile, hired me and Mane-Eac for support on a hack. And, by support, I mean we did all the heavy lifting while he supplied the tools and unsolicited advice. I think it was a fairly rudimentary gig, like changing the titles on property or the like. I mainly remember that Mane-Eac and I knocked it out and were downing shot after shot with Epic_Chaos at a dive bar on the other side of town well before the Happy Hour crowds.

The bar was called F.M's. When I asked the bartender what that stood for, he shrugged and fed the iguana that was in a tank right next to the cash register. The afternoon sun was blinding me through the front glass windows, so I took to staring at the bored reptile as it ate.

Hell, we were drinking so early in the day that the bartender attempted to kick us out. "We close for an hour from three to four," he said. Epic_Chaos kicked his head back and laughed as he slid two crumpled hundred-dol-

lar bills toward the barkeep. After he pocketed the money, the bartender placed a bottle of brown liquor straight out of Kentucky in front of us and said, "Well, I don't get paid for the next hour, but you guys can keep the place going while I'm gone."

He locked the door as he left, and we continued destroying our livers. I'd noticed Epic_Chaos cozying up to Mane-Eac around the fourth or fifth shot of our private bottle. I think it was more inebriation than attraction, but maybe I'm the jealous type. His perfectly pressed seersucker shirt and brown khakis made him look like a storefront mannequin to me. Plus, he clearly was wearing too much of a cologne that I couldn't quite place, but I'm pretty sure it had an animal or something nautical on the bottle.

With that much liquid courage coursing through his veins, Epic_Chaos probably thought he was twelve feet tall and bulletproof. Mane-Eac's a beautiful woman and all that, but this type of behavior was very unprofessional in my opinion, even if we completed the job. My protective side wanted to say something, but she's no damsel in distress. While the shots slurred her voice and glassed her eyes, she'd done a fine job of deflecting every advance Epic_Chaos shot her way. When he put his hand on her thigh, she removed it. When he pinched her butt, she slapped his face. Each time, he shook it off, almost as if this was a game to him.

Unfortunately, only half of the gig's payment was in our accounts at this point, but I had no problem investing the rest in supporting Mane-Eac's dignity if she went off. I mean, who wouldn't gladly lose ten grand to watch a preppy get his ass kicked?

The problem was that me, Mane-Eac, and Epic_Chaos were shooting straight whiskey. One of the principal ingredients in whiskey is a malted rye. Regular rye can prevent gallstones and lower your blood pressure. Malted rye can raise your blood pressure and increase your anxiety in some individuals, which is why you see everything from shouting matches to bar fights to grown men openly crying after consuming several shots of brown liquor.

In others, consuming rye has the opposite effect: it brings on the Sandman and his deep slumbers. Which is exactly what was happening to Mane-Eac. Her yawns got longer and more frequent. Her eyelids were heavy garage doors that kept closing and opening, though they were staying shut longer the more shots we consumed.

The preppy licked his lips as his eyes traced every inch of her body. "How about I help you home?" asked Epic_Chaos as he hopped up from his bar stool and forced his left hand under her right arm. "Even though it is daylight, it's not safe for a pretty thang like you."

With closed eyes and her head rotating side to side like a little bobble-head, she smirked. "All I need is to pee!"

"Well, I can certainly help there," he said. As she rested her head on his shoulder and he gave her noggin a kiss, the last thing he was suspecting was me. I yanked him around so fast he dropped Mane-Eac on the dirty wood floor.

"Hey, man, what the hell?" asked Epic_Chaos.

"Look, dude, the type of help you're offering her, she ain't asking for." At least that was what I thought I said: the whole sentence came out in one garbled take, like I had a mouthful of marbles or something.

"What's it to you, loverboy?" asked Epic_Chaos.

Before I could retort, Mane-Eac yelled from her spot on the floor, "Boys-boys-boy-yoz! Shuddap and let me go pee."

As I reached down to lift her up, she grabbed my right arm with her left hand. Her right hand was balled up as Epic_Chaos hooked his arm through hers. When we reached the bathroom door, I was so focused on helping Mane-Eac through that I discounted Epic_Chaos's determination.

The door was wide enough for one person to slip through. It appeared to be a single stall type bathroom, complete with one lightbulb and ugly-ass green tile. I thought us two guys would sort of shimmy Mane-Eac into the bathroom and shut the door for her. Epic_Chaos had other ideas.

In one movement, Epic_Chaos slipped into the bathroom and pushed me backwards. The sudden shift in balance forced me to let go. After I hit the ground, I heard the bathroom door latch click and echo in the empty bar.

All the alcohol in my system burned bright red as I banged on the door. I remember hearing a jumble of words as I slammed my shoulder into the center of it, hoping that the door was cheap and hollow. As far as my body could tell, they made it out of the same material as Captain America's shield because it would not budge.

The ruffling sound of clothes falling preceded a sharp metal ting that hit the air: a belt buckle connecting with the bathroom's tile. Realizing I was too hammered to pick the lock, I kicked the bronze doorknob at an angle, hoping it would shatter. After four kicks that sent lightning up my spine, I heard a scream so high pitched I thought Epic_Chaos was murdering Mane-Eac.

"Mane-Eac!" I screamed as I let loose a full body kick, the kind where you whip your body back and slam everything into your heel, and the door opened at the same time. My kick caught Epic_Chaos dead in the chest as he hobbled out of the bathroom in a bloody mess.

However, he acted like I hadn't just put all of my effort into a stomp as he tilted his head toward the bathroom and yelled, "You bitch! I'll kill you!"

In the bathroom, I saw a bloody pocketknife in Mane-Eac's right hand and what appeared to be a crumpled-up piece of bloody roast beef in the other.

Epic_Chaos grabbed his coat and passed the bartender as he unlocked the front door.

When the barkeep saw the blood on Epic_Chaos and then Mane-Eac with a bloody knife, he shook his head and muttered, "Not my monkey, not my circus," and headed back behind the bar.

Without uttering a word, Mane-Eac and I took our old seats at the bar, still leaving an empty spot for our client. The barkeep refilled our empty shotglasses. Mane-Eac's shaking, bloody hands lifted the brown liquor and toasted the empty seat. I raised mine as well.

"To Epic_Chaos," said Mane-Eac. "My first successful circumcision."

We clinked our tiny glasses and downed the liquor. The barkeep picked up Epic_Chaos' glass, washed it, and filled the three glasses. He raised a shot, and we all followed.

"To weird shit on a Tuesday."

We all clinked and downed the whiskey. The barkeep wandered over to the bathroom, opened the door, and whistled. "Police?" he asked.

We shook our heads.

"Alrighty," he said as he opened the door that read Janitor and grabbed a mop and bucket.

We sat in silence for a while. I didn't know whether to apologize for letting Epic_Chaos get the jump on me or to ask what happened or to change the subject entirely.

"My father gave me this knife," Mane-Eac finally began as she held the pocketknife with the blade's point resting on the bar as she turned it around and around. The faded white words Tuff Nut against a red background in some kind of sideways font caught my eye. "It was his father's first. Some trinket from a Crackerjack box or something. Dad first taught me how to sharpen it with spit and stone. Said you've gotta understand what strengthens and supports your tools before you use them. Then he taught me how to hold it, depending on the task. Stabbing and cutting are two completely different grips. Yeah, he made me kill a rabbit with it when I was ten. Sure, it was traumatic, but he said that it would fortify me for when, not if, I had to use it for protection."

"Your father was a smart man," I said.

"In some ways, yeah," she countered, then dropped the blade into a nearby glass of water. "I didn't always carry this, you see." She sighed as she mumbled the words, "And sometimes a knife is just not enough."

"I'm sorry I couldn't get the door open," I blurted out, as if the words were hot air that required escape from my lungs.

"That's not on you, because I don't need saving, Tanto." After the clear liquid had turned pink, Mane-Eac fished out the knife and dried the blade and hilt with a paper napkin.

"There was a time…" She cleared her throat and took three breaths before she spoke again. The only sound in the room was the water pouring from the mop bucket. "There was a time I really needed this knife, and I didn't have it. And that little girl would've given anything for someone like you to kick open that door. So, don't you dare beat yourself up for trying, Tanto. Don't you ever take on the burden for attempting the right thing. There aren't many do-gooders like you out there. Don't let this world change that about you."

With one shot of alcohol left in the bottle, I split it between our two glasses and raised mine.

"To fighting the good fight," I said.

Mane-Eac responded, "I'll always drink to that."

We downed the drinks and headed towards the door. Before we even turned the knob, the bartender cleared his throat.

Shit. The bill.

I reached for my wallet, but Mane-Eac swatted my hand away.

"I've got this, because I just cost us ten grand."

"Twenty."

"Asshole."As she put down three hundred dollars, it is only then that I noticed she still held part of Epic_Chaos's member in her other hand. With a smile, she dropped it in the iguana's tank as we left. My last memory of that place was of that iguana's tongue snatching that bloody skin and swallowing it without a second thought.

Chapter Twenty-Four

My Phone

Almost on cue, the soldiers yank both of our hoods off and return my thoughts to our current predicament. The bright lights in our eyes come not from flashlights, but from standing lamps. The kind you see in a photo shoot, or a beheading.

"You know, when my boss told me to bring in some perps to appease the Attorney General's boner for black hat hackers, I told him it would be a walk in the park," she says as she flicks some dirt from under her fingernails. I want to correct my captor by saying *lady boner*, since the Attorney General is female, but the angel on my shoulder holds my tongue.

Michelle strolls right in front of us, doing that slow heel-to-toe strut police officers do in the movies. The kind of walk that accentuates each step, almost gloating that she can walk while we are bound. She now wears a bulletproof vest, and a flipped lanyard. I can't read all of it, but it certainly looks official. All I can make out is the top part, possibly the department she works for: *C.B.—Mercator Agency*, and the words *Per Legem Directam.*

Those initials, department name, and saying all mean jack squat to me, unfortunately. Except that they're the ones who are going to either arrest me or kill me.

Maybe she's hiding her name on purpose. This one move tells me she knows this capture isn't clean. If she were a weather pattern, I'd call her sunny with a chance of thunderstorms.

"My gut tells me, though, that you somehow knew this was a trap," Agent Michelle says. "What tipped you off?"

"The RV next door," answers Mane-Eac. "Yes, you did a good job of putting down gravel to cover up any tracks and to cover up the ethernet cable that connects these computers to the ones in the van. But, I mean, if you're going to use it as a command center, at least flatten the tires. Sheesh. That's some rookie junk there. Any abandoned jalopy like that would have four bald and empty ones on rusted rims outside this joint. There's more air in those tires than in the Goodyear blimp."

"Uh-huh," says Michelle as she strolls between us, popping her knuckles. I can't tell if that is a power move or a nervous one. Maybe both. "And you, Mr. Marigold."

I don't want to incriminate myself further by speaking without a lawyer present, but I still need to buy us some time.

"I had my suspicions when you showed me the bank statement and your checkbook. The numbers didn't link up."

"Huh," says Michelle, biting her bottom lip. "Way back then?"

"Seems like only yesterday."

"Then, why, knowing this was a trap, did you take the gig?"

"It's like you said at the beginning: DJ's just a damn kid that got curious. He didn't cause any damage. He should not have to spend the rest of his life in jail."

"So, what, you thought that we'd let you actually hack our systems from under our noses and you'd use it against us? That you'd willingly walk into a trap and then get away with it?"

Sort of. That is exactly why we sped up the deadline for this hack. When we took twenty-four hours off the table, it allowed for our potential captors to make minor mistakes. Such as leaving air in those tires.

"I want to call my lawyer," I say. This won't happen. I know that cyberterrorism crimes are relatively new in the judicial system: just recently they changed the label on what I do from *electronic civil disobedience* to *cyberterrorism*, which is why arrested hackers don't always get representation. When you're dying of thirst, it can't hurt to ask for water.

"That's not going to happen," counters Michelle as she grabs a chair from in front of a computer. She flips it around and straddles the rusty metal, her arms over the top of it. It's a power move, a pure confidence pose.

One that's belied by the nervous way she's rubbing her hands together.

"We have enough to put you down in a deep, dark hole for eternity." She smiles.

I'm sweating, partially because of the situation, but moreso because those lamps are producing desert-level heat.

"Now, I'm willing to put in a good word with my boss, but you have to give me something."

Ah. Here's the part where the feds expect you to beg and plead and bargain and rat on everyone you've ever known. Nothing good ever comes from selling your soul to the Feds. They take you in, break you down, stick a giant straw in your soul, suck out every bit of useful info they can, and then send you on your way, empty yet alive.

I give Agent Michelle a show, not a source. For the next few minutes, I cry. I scream. Mane-Eac gets in on it too. We rock back-and-forth and moan like we just saw someone shoot Old Yeller. We even threaten to rat on each other; anything to buy more time.

It is one hundred percent a ruse because, for this to even have a sliver of a chance of success, there must be no doubt. For this to work, we need a few more minutes for something that has saved my ass every single time someone put me in cuffs.

Overwhelming reasonable doubt.

"I'll tell them about the time you hacked all the rides at Disneyland just so you could skip to the front of the line," Mane-Eac says, screaming and yet trying not to laugh. I notice the nervousness in her voice, that underlying tremor. But I know she's a professional. She's got this.

"Oh, well, I'll tell them how you shot J-J-John F. K-Kennedy!" I counter as I stutter through a chuckle. That stutter comes out sometimes when I'm nervous as well. I hope Agent Michelle mistakes it for humor.

"I wasn't even born then, you idiot!"

"Well, I'm talking about what you did in a p-p-past life."

"Oh, you wouldn't dare!"

"Oh, I would! I would!"

It might be gallows humor, but it is almost all we have.

Almost.

Somehow, Michelle slaps both of us in under a full second. "Shut up!"

Good. Violence as a response is a last resort.

In my mind, I can hear the ice that Agent Michelle stands on, her perfect little trap, cracking.

Even though my cheek burns and my mouth waters from the impact, the moment Mane-Eac and I make eye contact, we laugh.

"Why the hell are you laughing?"

I breathed deep after a few more snickers. "If you're not going to let me make a call, then you should at least look at my cellphone."

"I thought you didn't own one."

"I got one for this very occasion, Agent Michelle," I said in my most uptight accent. "I hope you feel honored."

That joyful, proud light in Michelle's green eyes has shifted.

Uncertainty. And there is nothing a federal agent hates more than that. Her furrowed brow and darting eyes make it look like Agent Michelle is the one in zip-tie handcuffs.

"Someone hand me the evidence bag," she commands.

"Ma'am, there is no phone in the evidence bag."

Not believing the soldier, Michelle breaks the seal on a clear evidence bag. Everything she's doing now is technically evidence tampering. Agent Michelle doesn't care. That is not the lone piece of evidence in our case. It is only an ancillary piece to her.

To Mane-Eac and myself, it is as precious as Tolkien's *The One Ring.*

"Alright, smart guy, where is your phone?"

I say nothing and hold my smile. She slaps it clean off my face, but the dramatic pause is worth the taste of copper in my mouth.

"You should really check the closet over there."

Agent Michelle motions for someone to get to the closet. Whoever gets there says something so useful that it makes me wish I could put them on my Christmas Card list as a thank you.

"Ma'am, do you mean this phone that is hooked into the hardline?"

Agent Michelle opens her mouth, then shuts it and glares at me.

"What the hell did you do?"

I tilt my head back towards the locker. I can't make eye contact with the soldier, but I do say, "It's fine to unhook it now."

In a few seconds, Agent Michelle holds the smartphone under my nose.

"Again, what the hell did you do?"

I really want to smile again, but too much bluffing is a bad thing, so I answer, "You should really read that incoming message."

"There's no signal in here." She points at the zero bars on my phone. "There's no way you have an incoming message."

"Check the time on it."

If this was a horror movie, the expression on Michelle's face is as if she just got a text that reads *the killer is in the room with you*.

"This is bullshit."

It is bullshit, fresh from the bull's ass. Completely fabricated bullshit. I changed the clock on the phone right before I plugged it in. Hopefully, Agent Michelle's focus is on the time of the message and fails to notice that the phone is several hours off from our current time.

"Anything is possible," I say. That kind of smartass response is just one of the many stupid things I often do: project my pride. Pride might be a deadly sin, but at least it is mine.

Deception is at the heart of hacking. Many a Bushido warrior dressed up to sneak past an armed guard. Look, even the sumo wrestler-sized Benkei, a warrior monk who had defeated nine hundred and ninety-nine samurai, was ultimately bested by a Bushi dressed in drag and playing a flute.

As she rolls the dongle attached to the end of the phone between her fingers, her expression changes. The look of concern on Agent Michelle's face shifts, for just a second, from anger to flat out fear, before she refocuses.

"Tech, get over here!"

From his seated position, a nerdy guy in reading glasses and body armor stumbles towards Michelle and bumps into her. He's as used to wearing tactile gear as a child playing dress-up in mama's high heels.

Michelle hands him the phone and dongle.

He says, "Whoa…", in the same tone that a surfer would say when he sees an impressive wave. "And why is there a screenshot of a completely empty hard drive?"

"Don't *whoa* me, is it possible to connect to the internet with this thing?"

The tech's eyes dart between the cable and the actual smartphone. As he scrolls through the software installed on there, he fidgets with the cable in his other hand. Most of the pieces of software I have on there have one thing in common: they are hacking tools.

Now, if I only knew how to play the flute…

"StarTech's a good company, man," says the Tech, examining the hardware. "This thing has a bunch of black hat software on it, and, cool, I haven't seen one of these before and, look, it's spliced with a DermLite adapter, never would've thought to do that…"

"Speak English and tell me if this thing can connect through a phone line."

"Um, I'm not sure, but theoretically, it's built that way…"

"Is there a way to check it?"

"I wouldn't know how."

Silence fills the air. The tech shifts from foot to foot, a child waiting for his teacher to give him an assignment.

Technically, I have zero idea how to set up that burner phone so that it will transmit on a limited access phone line like the one that goes into the fire detection system. All I am shooting for is the Tech's doubt, because enough doubt might get us out of this jam.

Or it might get us shot in the head.

"If you don't believe me," I say, taking the initiative, "then take a look at the incoming and outgoing traffic to your servers. Let me know if you find anything…amiss."

The tech darts back to his laptop. Two minutes of clickity-clacks go by before he yells what I hoped he would.

"Um, there's been a lot of traffic on the site. I mean, like, an attack, and maybe an attempted breach."

"Are you kidding me?"

"Um, no." More clickity-clacks fill the room's silence until he speaks again. "Hey, um, also, you know all those files that they were going after in our simulation?"

"Yes..."

Never has the word yes sounded so painful.

"They're gone."

No, they're there. You're just looking at what we want you to look at.

I almost say something, but the Bushido have a story about winning without fighting: the key is to let the other warrior sabotage himself.

"There's no way that Mr. Marigold here could hack our servers using a damned cellphone on a damned ancient phone line."

"I agree," I say. "That was the way I contacted our courier."

"What courier?"

"The question isn't *what courier*, but *why a courier*?" I turn my attention to Mane-Eac. "Do you remember the Charlie Brown Pez dispenser, Ms. Magnolia?"

"Do you mean the one that had a flash drive installed with a keylogger program on it so it could record our progress?" says Mane-Eac.

"That's the one. Say, where is it now?"

"Wow, I guess it got flushed when I went to the bathroom."

"Huh, toilets are just so useful. I wonder if the feds thought that it would be easier to set up a simulation that runs exactly like their real security."

"Oh, that would be so much easier, and take a lot less time," she says in a mock tone. "I wouldn't even consider wasting time on creating anything else since I was already one hundred percent sure about the code not leaving this room."

"I was wondering if someone thought to stop the outgoing pipes for flushed contraband."

"Well, if they didn't, that's some, as Charlie Brown would say, *good grief*."

"Good grief, indeed."

"There is no way that you two got that out of here," says Michelle.

In a fury, she lifts the battering ram and shuffles with the thirty-pound rod into the bathroom. In four moves, she shatters the toilet from bowl to base.

There, among the spraying water and porcelain rubble, she finds a lone Adderall pill, but no Pez dispenser. Agent Michelle holds it in her hand like the cyanide pill that will kill her career.

Before she gets any ideas, I say, "If it would help, please take my phone outside and get a signal. I'm willing to bet any questions you have will answer themselves then."

Chapter Twenty-Five

Plausible Deniability

Around thirty minutes pass. I can't be sure because I can't see the clock on the wall since Agent Michelle shoved the hoods back on us when she went outside. We are still pretty screwed. So far, everything I've said and done is eighty percent bluff. I'm hoping the twenty percent of truth saves us.

During her time outside, Agent Michelle has played the same video again and again because I hear the same yelling part at the beginning five times. I know the footage by heart.

On the video, Agent Michelle and whoever else watches it with her, can see the poor custodian we *knocked out* holding the Charlie Brown Pez dispenser.

They can also hear him saying the following: Hello! Hey there, remember me? I fool you. I'm not New Yorker. I'm from Kazakhstan, baby. My accent. You like? Robert DeNiro in Taxi Driver. Hey! It is me you are tawk'n to. Hey! I practice. Look, thank you for this keylogger. Also, thank you for setting up the simulation like real firewall. Much easier, yes? So, in one hour, I release files we take on The Web of Dark, unless you let everyone go. Okay, bye-bye. Go Mets!"

The actual custodian we discussed kidnapping yesterday mysteriously called in sick when he found himself fifty-thousand dollars richer. All he had to do was give us his RFID card and cough on his answering machine message. I sure hope that money will help with his medical bills.

Good Ole Sagdiyev Kalashnikov. When you drink large amounts of vodka with a person, you gain their trust. That is why he willingly filmed that video and sent it to me. And why he didn't mind getting tased and drugged with a canister of CO2 and not actual knockout gas. All that CO2 did was give him a sore throat, probably.

I was worried that Squirrel_Lord would recognize him. Thankfully, Sagdiyev has lost over fifty pounds and shaved his head since the last time we all worked together. A further problem is Sagdiyev filmed that video yesterday on this burner phone. I took that cellphone from his pocket when I grabbed the RFID card after our auto accident. It is the one in Agent Michelle's hands right now. As for what was flushed, Sagdiyev has an *in* with the right people at Miami-Dade Water and Sewer Department. He'll have access and filter points that the average person never even thinks of when they flush their waste. Even so, the odds of Sagdiyev finding the right sewer line and the Pez dispenser, complete with a recording of all the keystrokes necessary to bypass at least one Federal firewall, without it getting trapped en route, are astronomical. Knowing Sagdiyev, he has a team scouring the sewers right now and might even find the Pez dispenser within a day or so, but that's an unknown we could not risk.

As for the blank servers, well, that too is a decoy. The high traffic on the servers is true. Sagdiyev and his crew just attacked that firewall like it was an all-you-can-drink vodka buffet. They might even have gotten through.

That is a major unknown, so that is why I downloaded that piece of code from the Pez dispenser onto the simulation servers. It is so tiny, but so necessary, because it brings up a decoy screen that hijacks the tech's search parameters when he looks for the U.S. Attorney's files.

Everything hinges on a breeze not hitting this house of cards until we get free. I have one more layer on this stack that might keep us out of jail.

Agent Michelle reenters and yanks the hoods from our heads. Her flushed cheeks and hunched over posture, more direct than defeated, tells me everything I need to know.

She's about to show she's in charge.

She points at Squirrel_Lord and yells, "Okay, the deal is off with this one. Get him out of here."

"Wait, what?" Two soldiers zip-tie him and haul his double-crossing ass out the front door. "We had a deal!"

"Not with me, you didn't."

I almost feel sorry for Squirrely. As least, about as sorry as mice might feel for a cat stuck in a tree.

As they drag him out, the look he sends me could knock down a wall.

"For this, before I kill you, I will destroy you first!" he shouts as he's dragged away.

I laugh, mainly because that line feels like it comes straight out of an 80s action movie.

Once he's gone, Michelle whips out a knife and flicks open the blade. She cuts my restraints, then returns to the front and lobs it at my chest.

Out of instinct, I catch it.

"Shit!" Too late, I drop the blade; my fingerprints are on the weapon.

"And look who just tried to escape," she says as she pins me against the wall. I put my hands up, but Agent Michelle is not interested in taking anyone alive at this point.

"Michelle, don't—"

She punches me in the stomach. I double over as my gut roars and bile hits the back of my throat.

The sound of a Glock chambering a round echoes.

"Wait…hold up…"

Agent Michelle yanks my head up, grabs my trachea, and squeezes. My mouth inadvertently opens. She shoves her pistol so deep in my throat it hits my tonsils. I gag and my instinct is to grab the gun, to remove the foreign object in my body.

But she's counting on that. My fingerprints at a certain angle on that gun will show forensics I tried to get the gun away from her.

I know the truth: no one in this room will stop her from pulling the trigger. A dead hacker is better than one that can give a statement that shows how much Agent Michelle has screwed up this slam dunk of an arrest. She's in rage and focused on the short term instead of looking at all the Feds can gain from this arrest. The worst-case scenario is that they write this up like I was trying to grab a gun and got shot. Multiple gun shots to my head will skew any forensics in favor of the living.

And, once I'm dead, they won't leave Mane-Eac alive as a witness.

"We will find the drive. Even if we don't, you will go down for this hack. Your value alive just hit zero."

I try to talk, but all that comes out is gibberish. The taste of gun oil causes my mouth to salivate. Drool dribbles down my chin as my hands go wide.

"Don't do it!" yells Mane-Eac. She stands and rushes head long at Michelle. A soldier easily intercepts her and yanks her away. "Don't!" A black leather glove covers her mouth. The soldier drags her out of my sight.

A smile crosses Agent Michelle's lips. The other agents look away. If they don't see this play out, they don't have to lie under oath.

Plausible deniability.

Chapter Twenty-Six

Everything is About to Change

In the split seconds that remain in my life, only the Tech in the background still looks my way.

He is my only hope.

As Agent Michelle's index finger dances across the trigger, I shoot out my fingers in numerical sequence. I imagine the light sounds of my knuckles popping and digits flicking echoes in the room, but I'm sure no one else can hear them.

He's a coder, he must understand I am sending a message.

Sweat streams into my eyes. Agent Michelle angles the barrel up in my mouth, guaranteeing she doesn't just blow out my throat. One bullet, straight through my brain.

I keep popping numbers from my fingers like they are a magical spell that will save our lives, because they are our only hope.

"Goodbye, Mr. Marigold."

In my mind, I hear the gunshot. I picture my body falling to the ground. I don't see loved ones greeting me or see my life flash before my eyes. All I picture is nothingness.

"Wait…"

The squeaky voice of a nerdy angel comes from the back of the room. "Six-nine-five-four-and then some numbers I missed."

I shake my hands and start the sequence again. After each number, the Tech recites the numbers. I could attempt the second sequence, but I worry about confusing the Tech. This is my last card; I only get to play it once.

In those angry, green eyes of Agent Michelle, her pupils go from small to large for a split second. There is no change in the room's lighting.

That's recognition in her eyes.

"Hold up…I know that number somehow…"

She yanks the Glock from my mouth so fast that the front sight chips my front tooth. I run my tongue over the new jaggedness and swallow the sliver.

Then, I answer Agent Michelle's unspoken question when I spout out two series of ten numbers apiece.

Then I wait.

Agent Michelle points the pistol in her hand towards the ground. I watch as she chews the inside of her cheek, deep in thought. Without saying a word, she shoves me to the ground, grabs her cellphone, and steps outside.

My breathing goes from hyperventilating to gasping. I control my breathing because I'm no good to anyone unconscious.

The hum of computers fills the silence. Apparently released by a soldier, Mane-Eac returns to my side. Her eyes bounce from side to side as she eloquently asks about the elephant in the server room as she whispers, "What the ever-loving hell did you just do?"

"Played…the…backup plan…"

"Wait…we had a backup plan?"

My mind races faster than a rocket. I'm not sure if this worked. Or if it worked too well and Agent Michelle was going to shoot both of us for hedging our bets.

If she shoots us though, then our insurance policy will guarantee her own failure as well.

Mutually assured destruction at its finest.

I'm not sure how much time passes. I may have even passed out, because the next thing I know, I hear a scream. It's not one of just pain or frustration. It is more of a wail; one you'd expect from a rat caught in a trap. One that mixes shock with defeat.

From outside the front door comes Michelle's voice. Once booming, now it sounds so small, tired, and short of breath.

"Cut them loose..."

"Ma'am, are you serious?" asks one of the armed soldiers. "Look, we just..."

"Now!"

A soldier cuts Mane-Eac's bindings. Another ushers both of us towards the door.

Once outside, Agent Michelle sends daggers from her eyes my way.

"You arrogant, stupid, son of a bitch."

I keep quiet. We still don't have what we came here for.

"What the hell did you just do?"

I let that question linger in the air like a child's helium balloon floating away from its grasp.

Only after the rage tremors settle in Michelle's body and she holsters her firearm, do I dare speak.

"Reduce DJ's sentence, those numbers disappear. They are only pending because they take seven days to process. However, you better believe multiple screenshots and statement logs of both accounts have already been made and are more backed up than an ass in the club."

"The kid's getting life. The Attorney General wants an example made."

"Thirty days. County, not federal time. The kid didn't do anything but trespass."

"No way." A taut line runs her jaw, like she is thinking about her next move. "He broke through government firewalls. That's federal. Thirty years."

"Six months. House arrest. Take it or leave it."

Her finger traces the holstered gun's grip. "Are you willing to die here to prove your damn point?"

I lean forward. "Are you willing to go to jail to prove yours?"

This scorn behind Agent Michelle's eyes burns my soul. I hate doing this, but it had to be done. Agent Michelle's teeth are so clenched that I hear her jaw pop.

"I'll need to make a call."

"You can use my phone if you want to save a dime."

Stupid pride, I scold myself. *I couldn't just let that go, could I?*

"Okay, what the hell is going on?" Mane-Eac asks after Michelle stomps off.

With the guards flanking me, I whisper in her ear, "When Michelle approached us, she showed me a checking account statement and a checkbook. The feds set up one of those accounts to prove that there was money available to pay for our hack. Now, the other checkbook, well, those numbers went to another account. My guess was that the other account was Michelle's personal one."

"Wait, you memorized the check numbers, routing numbers, and branch bank of both accounts by just glancing at them?"

Mane-Eac takes my silence as my answer.

"I equally hate and love your smart brain." Her eyes dart around the room as she assembles her question. "So, what, you stole the money in all the accounts?"

"Worse."

From outside, I hear Agent Michelle apologizing over and over to someone on the phone. She speaks in stutter steps, trying to get in as many words as possible before the person on the other end of the phone, probably her boss, counters. After each barrage, she appears to shrink an inch, her body collapsing back in on itself.

"In the last four hours, there have been a series of very large deposits into those accounts," I say. "These deposits allegedly link back to Dancy Bear."

"...I have...heard of them..." The gears behind Mane-Eac's eyes turn faster. "They are Russian hackers, aren't they?"

My raised eyebrows answer that question.

"So, let me get this straight." Mane-Eac's pursed lips turn into a smile. "In the last few hours, someone deposited a large amount of money into both a federal account and the personal account connected to a federal agent. And that money is traceable to a Russian hacker group. Coincidentally, on the same day, a major government facility was recently attacked by a series of hacks and, if our Ukrainian friend has found the Pez dispenser, then there has been or will be an actual breach of a government firewall. And, if this information were to leak to the press and be spun in just the right manner, then it would appear that Russian hackers paid off one division of the U.S. government, and its agent, to gain access to another one's servers."

"Allegedly."

"Oh, of course." The smile crossing her face could light up a room. "Allegedly."

In the State of Florida, it is illegal to make a withdrawal from someone else's account. However, with an account number and name of the branch and bank and just the right amount of finesse, you can *deposit* almost anything into anyone's account without their knowledge or permission.

God bless loopholes, and that the U.S. government doesn't care how much money goes out of your account; just how much money comes in and where it comes from.

"It's done," says Michelle, re-entering the room and pocketing her cellphone. "Now what?"

"Now, we leave. You don't prosecute us. You don't pursue us. We are nothing more than a training exercise that results in a need for more training." I clear my itchy throat. "You let the dust on this settle, but you never forget that when you go after one of us, especially a kid, you go after all of us."

I say all of this with false confidence. Internally, I am shaking like a paint can mixer. I watch as Agent Michelle runs her index finger along the rubber grip of her holstered Glock 9mm.

Agent Michelle gets in my face.

"Starting today, you better run and never stop running," she shoves a finger so hard into my chest that I think she just stabbed my soul. "I'm coming for you. This sting was professional, clean. Then you made it personal. You might've gotten away with this one, but I will find you one day. I will hunt you down. And I will not kill you. Oh, no. I will throw you in a hole so deep that you'll keep falling for the rest of your life."

As Mane-Eac and I walk off towards the security guard's tower, my damned pride won't let me keep quiet. I pick up the duffel bag from the gravel and give it a squeeze as I yell out, “You can’t make a list if you don’t know my name.”

“Oh, I know just about everything about you…Tanto.”

Mane-Eac and I move off to collect the duffel bag and leave, but it’s with the sensation of an invisible fishing net covering my body. Every bit of joy from this successful hack, this liberation, shifts to a cold, body-numbing dread.

There is a story about a shogun, a commander, who captures his rival’s lover. To find out where his enemy is, the shogun tortures the woman psychologically. He lies to her and attempts to break her spirit. She cries and moans and the shogun thinks he has broken her. Only when she sings a beautiful song and warps his mind into freeing her and giving up his pursuit of her lover does he realize the shogun was never in control of the situation in the first place. While he held the trap, his prey snared him.

For the first time in my hacking career, I am now someone’s target. And, for the first time in my life, my brain and gut work in tandem to come to the conclusion I’ve always feared: everything is about to change.

THE END

Vengeance Arrives September 27, 2022

Tanto will return in *You Will Know Vengeance.*

A government plot. A con who holds all the cards. Can a young man protecting his fellow inmates stop a killer without losing his soul?

Skilled hacker Tanto finds inner quiet in the ways of Bushido. So, after SWAT drags him to a hidden compound to entrap other code jockeys, he spends the next eight years drawing on his inner strength to bring honor to his peers. But when the peaceful warrior takes a terrified and badly beaten newcomer under his wing, he's shaken to learn the kid was brutalized by an old nemesis.

As if things could not get worse, the same monstrous enemy lands in his cellblock. Now, Tanto fears for the tribe he's grown to love like family. And with the guards turning a blind eye to the rival's calculated atrocities, Tanto plans desperate measures that could trigger deadly results.

Can he maintain his sworn discipline and avoid leaving a bloody legacy?

***

To order your copy, please visit http://www.wapepperwrites.com/ywkv/

To read the first chapter of *YOU WILL KNOW VENGEANCE*, please continue reading.

Chapter 1 - Ice Cube on the Sun

The Feds give you zero notice when they kick in your door. There is no warning siren. There is no knocking on your door, which is soon to be shattered by a battering ram. There is only silence before the calculated chaos.

A loud crash awakens me, followed by what sounds like the rolling of tin cans along my hardwood floor. I jump out of bed just as a flash-bang touches my big toe. Out of the corner of my eye, I spot a drizzle of gray emitting from the smoke grenade atop my dirty laundry pile.

My thudding heartbeat fills my ears right before the explosion of the holy trinity of SWAT hand grenades—equal parts phosphorous, lightning, and thunder—floods my one-room apartment. I scream, but I cannot hear my own roar. Only my ringing ears, stinging eyes, and burning throat let me know I am still alive. The vibration of a stampede of footsteps shakes my body as leathery gloves assault my temporarily handicapable Helen Keller ass and shove me onto my bed, nose-first. The smells of rancid sheets and garlic fill my nostrils. A faceless assailant pins my arms behind my head and zip-ties my hands together. Then I am yanked to my feet.

The pure, white light blurring my eyes dims slightly. Through slitted eyes, I count six flashlights. Barrels of submachine pistols at the end of each beam of light are trained my way. I glance down and spot half a dozen lasers freckling my unshaven chest.

Four men rip all my electronics from the wall and bag everything. A man in a gas mask talks to me, but it's all a muffle of words, like I am talking to Charlie Brown's teacher. I nod. I do not know what I have agreed to. Soldiers exchange words. They pull something from a bag and march it my way.

The man closest to me shoves a hood over my head. My life as I know it melts away like it never existed.

I might as well have been an ice cube on the sun.

***

2010: Eight Years After Capture

(continued in *You Will Know Vengeance: A Tanto Thriller)*

To order your copy, please visit http://www.wapepperwrites.com/ywkv

Dedication

While this is a fictional story based around true events, one bit of truth stands out that the author wants to discuss. I wrote this short story in memory of a brilliant and inquisitive mind forced into an impossible situation. "DJ", the hacker known as DoGoodR, was a kid in the 1990's who successfully broke through the firewalls of several private businesses and government systems, all before he could legally drive an automobile.

There was never any proof that he was doing anything more than exploiting businesses' and governmental agencies' security shortcomings. According to court records, no damage was done, except for reputational damage by shining a light on the inadequacies of businesses and government agencies.

In today's world, people might call him a *white hat* or *gray hat* hacker because he did not break through these firewalls for any other reason than he could. His actions forced government agencies to improve their security and hire and train better computer security officers. However, in those early years of the Internet and Internet Security, DJ became one of the first federally sentenced juveniles for computer hacking. From this, he developed a lifelong depression. Further, a few years after his release, another hacker used the alias of "DJ" in a major department store hack.

Even though they arrested thirteen other hackers in connection to this particular crime, the U.S. government used this information as an opportunity to raid DoGoodR's home, his girlfriend's, and his sibling's, in search of any signs of illegal hacking or computer activity. They found nothing, yet DoGoodR wrote in a letter that they went after him because he was a "more appealing target."

The harassment of DJ ultimately resulted in his suicide. Suicide is a tragedy that impacts all of us. That is why a portion of this series' book sales will go to various Suicide Prevention Programs.

Thank you for reading and keep hustling wisely, Will

***

P.S. - Several of the stories in this tale that involve Bushido Warriors are sourced from the collection *Samurai Wisdom Stories: Tales from the Golden Age of Bushido* by Pascal Fauliot and Sherab Chodzin Kohn. The author highly recommends this collection to learn more about the Way of the Samurai, the Bushido Code in action, and tales to learn and live by.

***

Acknowledgements

First and foremost, I must thank God for blessing me with the opportunity to not only write, but to share my writing. Secondly, I would like to thank my wife and publisher Taddy for believing in me and guiding me (and our business) in a million different ways. In addition, I would like to thank the following people who contributed to this work currently in your hands:

· Developmental Editor Meaghan Wagner

· Proofreader David Sandretto

· Our Beta Readers team of Josi D., Kenneth M., Richard D., and Skye S.

Thank you to everyone who helped create this story!

Glossary (aka Jargon)

The following is a glossary of technical terms in this book. Some of these terms exist in the real world. Their definitions are drawn from multiple sources on the Internet (Wikipedia, Techopedia.com, Dictonary.com, HowToGeek, etc.) Other terms only exist in this book series. This is not an all-inclusive list and will continue to grow. For further definitions, please visit our website at HustleValleyPress.com.

Alviss – a proprietary private messaging application (also the name of the author's favorite locksmith).

Anti-Virus – (of software) designed to detect and destroy computer viruses.

Basic Input Output System (aka BIOS) – code that instructs a computer on how to perform basic functions such as system booting and input controls.

Bay, The – historically, Guantanamo Bay was a place where people viewed by the United States of America as "enemies of the State" or "combatants" were incarcerated and interrogated. The author is unsure if this site officially continues its prior function.

Blog – a regularly updated website or web page, typically one run by an individual or small group, that is written in an informal or conversational style.

Bot (aka Robot) – an autonomous program on the internet or another network that can interact with systems or users.

Buffer (aka Buffering) – a temporary memory area in which data is stored while it is being processed or transferred, especially one used while streaming video or downloading audio.

Bug – an (intentional or unintentional) error in a computer program or system.

Bushi – a practitioner of the Way of the Samurai or the Bushido Code.

Bushido Code – the historic code of conduct for Japan's warrior classes, and the word "bushido" comes from the Japanese roots "bushi" meaning "warrior," and "do" meaning "path" or "way."

Captures – the successful online trapping of individuals on the Internet.

Catholic (in hacking) – attempting to break into a government or government connected server or series of servers.

CDs (aka Compact Discs) – a way to store data and music.

Chicken-Choker trap – an online trap where the victim is teased with something enticing and leads to his own capture by following his own (morbid) desires.

Coder eyes – a symptom of eye strain that occurs when the user spends too much time staring at a computer.

Compiler – a program that converts source code written in a programming language.

Dam Breaker – someone who breaks through firewalls.

Damascus – the forging of steel by heating, breaking, and reforming many times.

Dark Web – the part of the World Wide Web that is only accessible by means of special software, allowing users and website operators to remain anonymous or untraceable.

Davidson Protocol – a set of rules that allow prisoners to donate work/time off to another prisoner.

Disciplinary chips – devices that are installed into a human body, gain their power from the same source, and provide electrical shocks via remote control.

Emulator – software that enables one computer system (called the host) to behave like another computer.

Faraday (aka Faraday Bag) – a device that removes the ability to receive or transmit data from a device.

Firewall – a part of a computer system or network which is designed to block unauthorized access while permitting outward communication.

Flash drives – finger-sized devices that connect to a computer and have room for storage.

Gig – a job or task to which someone is promised something in return for completion.

Hack – use of a tool (such as a computer, person, device, or situation) to gain unauthorized access to data in a system.

Hacker – a person who uses computers to gain unauthorized access to data.

Hackers' Haven (aka Double-H) – a privatized prison that forces imprisoned hackers to hunt and secure other lawbreakers.

Hackvict – a convict that believes in using policy, action, or various forms of media to bring about political, economic, or social change.

Handle (aka Callsign or Username) – a person's identifier when they log into a computer and how the prisoners of Hackers' Haven are labelled.

HoneyBadger – a propriety operating system that uses components from both Linux and Windows operating systems.

Gakunodo – the tent where Bushido warriors rested; also, an efficient software that entices individuals online and records their (illegal) footsteps.

Internet Relay Chat (aka IRC) – a group communication device that uses text-based chats or instant messaging to correspond with individuals and share files.

IP Address – a unique string of characters that identifies each computer using the Internet Protocol to communicate over a network.

Keylogger – a computer program that records every keystroke made by a computer user, especially in order to gain fraudulent access to passwords and other confidential information.

Kills – see "Captures."

Kilobyte (aka KB) – a unit of memory or data equal to 1,024 (2^{10}) bytes.

Land line – a telephone that is hooked directly into a socket via a series of cords.

Lap count – an interval between online pings.

Linux – an open-source operating system modelled on Unix.

Liquid Ocular Display Interceptor System (aka LODIS) – a device that records human eye and body movement through a watery substance.

Log file – file extension for an automatically produced file that contains a record of events (such as user choices) from certain software and operating systems.

Loopback – a static IP address used for testing integrated microchips.

Looping – the ability to copy files of a target computer without slowing down noticeable bandwidth or computing speed.

Malware – software that is specifically designed to disrupt, damage, or gain unauthorized access to a computer system.

Megabyte (aka MB) – a unit of information equal to 2^{20} bytes or, loosely, one million bytes.

Memory – the part of a computer in which data or program instructions can be stored for retrieval.

Neural Net – a computer system modeled on the human brain and nervous system.

Nintendo Time – when using an electronic device, this is the sensation that time is going slower than it actually is in the real world.

NumLk – the number lock key is a part of a keyboard that allows the user quick access to numbers.

Omni-Viewer – the (monitored) software that allows the prisoners of Hackers' Haven access to the Internet and Dark Web.

Paratrenicha (aka "Crazy Russian Ants") – Paratrenicha species near pubens. Ants that eat electronics (they really exist).

Ping – query (another computer on a network) to determine whether there is a connection to it.

Pods (aka Med Pods) – full body sized machines that detect abnormalities and illnesses in individuals.

Portable Document Format (aka PDF) – a versatile file format created by Adobe that gives people an easy, reliable way to present and exchange documents – regardless of the software, hardware, or operating systems being used by anyone who view them.

POS – stands for piece of shit.

Program Lidocaine – A computer worm that, once entered into a computer system, slows the system down until the system crashes.

Radio Frequency Identification (aka RFID) – denoting technologies that use radio waves to identify people or objects carrying encoded microchips.

Random Access Memory (RAM) – a type of data storage used in computers that is volatile and erased when a computer is turned off.

Randomizer – a piece of software that scrambles data or information.

Reg – slang for regular or regular occurence.

Root – a user account with full and unrestricted access to a system.

Rootkit – a set of software tools that enable an unauthorized user to gain control of a computer system without being detected.

Scanner – a device that scans documents and converts them into digital data.

Scripts – slang for computer code.

SkipTrace – a piece of software that takes the actual distance from the ping's source, the time at each occurrence, the bandwidth downloaded and uploaded to various IP sources, and strength and number of Internet connected devices in a known area as well as the draw of power from the utility company to calculate a user's location.

Software Patch – a downloaded series of files that fix a bug in a piece of software.

Solo – a piece of software that does not interact with other software; a hack involving software (or a software system) that forbids the use of additional software.

Tamahagane – a way of making a Japanese sword. The word tama means "round and precious," like a gem, while the word hagane means "steel."

Terabyte (aka TB) – a unit of information equal to one million million (10^{12}) or, strictly, 2^{40} bytes.

Terminal – see workstation.

Test Program Set (aka TPS) Report – "a document describing the step-by-step process in which an engineer tests and re-tests software or an electronics system." This definition is courtesy of Mike Judge, former engineer and programmer for a subcontractor working on military jets and the creator of *Office Space.*

Theia – software that allows residents of Hackers' Haven access to the Dark Web.

Timed out – a period of inactivity has passed that causes a software program to shut down.

Torrent – a file-sharing protocol based on peer-to-peer (P2P) technology that allows vast numbers of users to connect and share content without having to rely on a single source for downloads.

Tracer bullet – a piece of computer code that follows the trail of another piece of computer code and estimates possible objectives.

Units – rewards for successful captures, can be redeemed for food, non-essentials, or parole.

Unix – a widely used multiuser operating system.

VHS – a video home system cassette that was used by domestic video recorders and camcorders.

Virtual Private Network (aka VPN) – an arrangement whereby a secure, apparently private, network is achieved using encryption over a public network, typically the internet.

Virus (aka Computer Virus) – a piece of code which is capable of copying itself and typically has a detrimental effect, such as corrupting the system or destroying data.

War Room – a classroom-style arrangement of computer workstations where captures and the prevention of hacks occur.

Windows – a widely used single user operating system.

Workstation – a computer monitor, keyboard, mouse, and computer connected to the servers and Internet.

Worm – a standalone malware computer program that relies on security failures and replicates itself in order to spread to other computers.

Zipped – a compressed file that consists of one or several other files.

About the Author

W. A. Pepper writes suspenseful thrillers. *You Will Know Vengeance* is his debut novel. He is an awarding-winning *USA Today, Wall Street Journal*, and *Amazon* Bestselling Author for his contribution to the business anthology *Habits of Success*. Under different names (and his real one of Will Pepper), he has published in multiple academic journals, interactive e-books, anthologies, and online. During the COVID-19 pandemic, he and his wife Taddy (plus their dog Danger) started the publishing house Hustle Valley Press, LLC. Through it, they published four e-books that have amassed over one hundred five-star reviews. Further, the husband-and-wife team donated the first six months of revenue from the sale of each of those books to charity; this resulted in thousands of dollars raised for the reader-selected charities that support racial equality,

COVID-19 relief, veteran affairs, and St. Jude Children's Hospital. He has a PhD in Management Information Systems or, as he calls it, Business Computing, from The University of Mississippi. Finally, he, his wife Taddy, and their dog Danger split their time between Colorado and Mississippi.

CONTACT INFORMATION

tiktok.com/@wapepperwrites

facebook.com/wapepperwrites

goodreads.com/wapepper

instagram.com/wapepperwrites

amazon.com/author/willpepper

Made in the USA
Columbia, SC
20 October 2024